THE MYSTERY OF TULLY HALL

THE MYSTERY OF TULLY HALL

By

Zöe Billings

Illustrated by Sarah King

2021

For Mum and Dad, and of course, to Barrie, who now lives in the pages.

My thanks to my dear proof readers who have assisted and advised throughout this first novel. Your help has been invaluable. Thanks also to Vincent Formosa, for helping me navigate the publishing world

Contents

Chapter One

How it all Began

It was raining. Running down the old warped windows in the science labs, the water matched the mood of the four children who, sitting on the tables with their feet up on stools, whiled away their break time before the bell rang for the mid-morning lessons.

James, the tallest and oldest of the four by a few months, sat fixing Liz's phone. "I don't know how you manage to fill its memory up so quickly," he teased, "It was only at Easter that I cleared it for you before." Liz, sat opposite, grinned sheepishly. "I just like to download free apps, and it is ages old," she replied, smiling widely as James returned her, now functioning, phone. "Thanks James, I'll be more selective from now on."

"You said that before," laughed James, whose brown eyes, seemed to always twinkle when he smiled.

Barrie, usually shortened to Bar by the others, was checking his emails for the tenth time that day and seemed distracted, his fair curly hair dropping forward as he frowned, while Jenny, looking at the window panes with her striking green eyes, wondered out loud why the glass in them was so uneven.

"It's because glass is a super-cooled liquid, not a solid, so over time it responds to gravity and sinks to the bottom," replied Liz, sounding very knowledgeable, looking over at the windows and wishing they didn't let quite so much of the cold weather through.

"Rubbish!" said James, "They just didn't make it as flat in the old days when those windows were made."

"It's not rubbish, I read it on the internet," retorted Liz.

"Then it must be true," replied James, rolling his eyes and winking at Jenny.

The four children were all pupils at Grey Owls Boarding School, an imposing red brick and stone Victorian building, set in the heart of Yorkshire. Surrounded by green fields and woodland, and set deep within its own grounds, it was an impressive sight, which was always a bit daunting for new pupils. Once settled in, children soon realised that it was just an aging building, with high ceilings and long, hard wood floored corridors that echoed when you walked down them, nothing to be frightened of. They were in the first year, and had formed an unlikely friendship group since being thrown together in September. Now, the thought of spending the long summer holidays split apart was making their spirits as damp as the British summer outside.

"Two more weeks of school," sighed Jenny, "then eight weeks with no bed-time lights-out. I enjoyed going home at Christmas and Easter, but this time; it just feels like we'll be apart forever! I'll be back down in Cornwall, Bar will be in Wales, James will be up in Newcastle, and only Liz will be left here in glorious Yorkshire." Jenny, James and Barrie were all boarders at Grey Owls, James having won a scholarship to attend. Liz, whose mother, Mrs Green was the head of History at Grey Owls, was a day pupil and the youngest of the four, not having yet turned 12. She was the smallest too, with blonde hair, brown eyes and light freckles across the bridge of her nose. Animal mad, she kept the others entertained with stories of her pets' latest antics, and longed, one day to be a vet. Barrie also like animals, and said he'd quite like to be a farmer, and Liz could tend to his stock.

Liz and James turned sorrowful faces to Jenny, muttering their agreement that it would be a long boring summer. Barrie didn't react and, looking over at him, the three children saw that he was engrossed reading something on his phone. Sensing that he was being watched Barrie looked up. "Sorry," he said in an apologetic tone, putting his phone back into his pocket, "I was waiting to hear from Dad, he's just emailed me."

"What's the news?" asked James, "Is it all going ahead?"

"It seems so," replied Barrie, "Nain wants to leave the farm to me, for Dad, Sarah, and little Katie to live in with me, and she's going to live in a little cottage further down the valley. That way, the farm is guaranteed to stay in her family and she can enjoy seeing it being a busy family home again."

"Your gran, sorry, nain, sounds lovely," said Liz, "Won't she miss living in the farm?"

"She will be there a lot I think," replied Barrie, "but it was just too much for her, it's been in her family for generations, I think that's what made her carry on for so long with it. Anyway, the little cottage is on the farmland, it was an old cattle barn 'til it was converted last year, so she's not far away. It looks like my summer will be spent moving house."

Barrie's mother, Nain's daughter had died in an accident when he was very young, and his dad had remarried a couple of years ago. He and his new wife, Sarah, who Barrie loved like a mother, had a baby daughter together, Katie.

"Bet it will be exciting, exploring new places," said James. "What is it like?"

"Well, there's the farm house, that's built of old grey stone. It's quite big but pretty draughty. Dad says he will have to sort out the windows before winter comes. There are a few outbuildings and barns, I don't know what's in those, they've been locked up for as long as I can remember. The land is on a hill with the farmhouse near the top. As it slopes down there is a small river which runs through it and continues down the valley. There's a rickety bridge which spans the upper most part of the river as the farmland runs down the other side of the river."

"A rickety bridge? Wow, that sounds like fun," said James who, growing up in a town, longed for open spaces.

"Go on," cut in Jenny, who was dying to hear all about the place "What else is there around?"

"There's an old stately home a bit further down," continued Barrie, "which the farm used to be part of years and years ago. We don't own that of course, but our land continues on the other side of the river past it. Nain's cottage, I think, is just down from the stately home at the end of our land."

"What will your parents do with all that land?" enquired Liz. "Your dad has a job already doesn't he?"

"Yes," replied Barrie, "Dad will stay with the software company he says, but Nain has rented the land out to a local farmer for his sheep and cattle for years, I guess it will just carry on. She says you can't do much with that type of land, but it does look nice."

"Can we look at it on Google Earth?" asked Liz, "I have the app on my phone," she continued, grinning at James

"Great idea," replied Barrie, but just he spoke, the bell rang for the end of break time, and the four children all trooped off for their mid-morning lessons.

Meeting again in the dinner hall at lunchtime, the four sat in a huddle all pouring over James' tablet, which he'd brought from his room to see the farm on. "It starts up here," explained Barrie, tracing his finger around a satellite image of some slate roofed buildings, "and then down here, across the little river, and along the other side down there."

"What's that huge building there?" asked Jenny, pointing at an area off to one side, as her shoulder length brown hair fell forward over the screen.

"That's the stately home, Tylluan Hall I think it's called, makes the farm look tiny doesn't it?" replied Barrie

"I don't know how you get your tongue around these words and names," said Jenny in awe, "I can remember Nain, as it's like the number nine, but I wouldn't know where to begin with that hall."

"The alphabet it just a bit different, see?" said Barrie, "Double f is f, because f is v. Y is u, u can be e, double d is th…" he tailed off as Jenny looked bewildered. She tried a few times with Barrie breaking the name down.

"Y is like uh, double l is tlh type of sound, and u sounds like e. so it's T-uh-tlh-e-an." Jenny valiantly tried again, causing great amusement to the others before she, James and Liz settled on calling it Tully Hall. "What does it mean?"

"Owl Hall," said Barrie, "It's been undergoing renovation for years. I think Nain said it was nearly finished, I know Sarah has been involved with it in some way."

"And what's this bit? Is it the river?" asked Liz, leaning over and running her finger down to a thin line that ran, winding, through the whole image.

"Yes," confirmed Barrie, "it isn't very wide at the top, where the wooden bridge is, but by the time it passes where Nain will live, it's at least eighteen feet wide."

The four fell silent as they all stared at the screen, imagining what sort of fun they could have there, exploring new places together.

"Wish I could help you move" said James, wistfully, collecting up their trays as the end of lunch bell rang out loudly. "Would certainly beat a boring summer at my house."

Barrie looked up at James, his eyes bright with excitement. "James, you're a genius!" he exclaimed "Pen y Bryn farm has masses of room, why don't you all come and stay with me for the summer? Then we wouldn't have to be split up." All four felt a shiver of excitement go down their spines, what a wonderful idea it was. The challenge would be getting the grown-ups to agree.

Chapter Two

Exciting Plans

A flurry of emails were sent that evening, along with a number of phone calls as each of the four tried desperately to enthuse their parents about their exciting plans. Barrie's dad was more than happy to take on the three extra children in theory, but as he said to Barrie, the timing could be better. "Where will they all sleep Bar?" he asked, vainly trying to get Barrie to see the error of his impulsive invitation. "We've not even got enough beds for you all, and Sarah and I are only moving in this week. What with the baby and everything," Barrie's dad paused as he sought the right words. Barrie was his number one son, as he often told him, with Barrie replying, with a wry smile every time, that he was his only son. "How about at the end of the summer, when we're all settled and you know the area better, surely that would make sense and you could then show the others places you enjoy?" "That's just it Dad," implored Barrie. "The whole point is that we explore the farm and places round it together, that's half the fun. I know my way around enough from holidays there. The others know it'll be a bit rough, they're fine with it Dad, please?"

"They might be ok with it Bar, but what about their parents? They need to be fully aware of the conditions, and I imagine they will want to have their children back home after being away all term." Barrie's father, thinking back to his own childhood of forming clubs and making adventures, was warming to his son's idea, hearing the excitement in his voice. His late wife, Barrie's mother, had always been exploring places. Like mother like son he thought. "See what the other parents think," he added, in a resigned but friendly tone, knowing when he was beaten. "If they're ok with it, fully informed mind, no painting this place to be the Ritz, then I'm sure we'll manage something."

"Oh Dad, thank you so so much, you're the best!" shouted Barry down the phone, "I'll go now and tell the others. Love you." Barrie tore out of his room and raced down the corridor to find James. "Barrie Williams!" boomed an angry voice "How uncharitable of you to leave the rest of us to succumb to the flames I presume you are running from."

"Sorry, Sir," uttered Barrie, horrified to find himself face to face with the tall, stern figure of the deputy head Mr Storm who, at a moment's notice could send Barrie back to his room to spend the evening in room detention, stopping him from speaking to the others. "No fire Sir, I'm sorry, Sir." That was the way to reply to Mr Storm, no excuses, no witty remarks, just be solemn and polite, contrite and brief.

"Hmmm," replied Mr Storm, "I should hope you are, I expect better from you." Barrie looked into the teacher's eyes, and Mr Storm saw in them no insolence to ignite his infamous temper, just sparkling blue, "Off you go. Walking."

"Thank you, Sir, and I apologise again," replied Barrie as he dropped his gaze and walked away towards James's room. Narrow escape, he thought as he tapped on James's door before diving inside.

James was sat cross legged on his bed, his phone to his ear, listening earnestly; he waved Barrie to the chair by his desk. All the rooms were the same at Grey Owls, plain and simple, a bed, a desk, and a wardrobe. James had added his personal touch to the room with a box of tools and electronics, used to fix other students', and occasionally teachers', devices, and some chemical structure models. Barrie examined the models with interest as James, unmoving, made noises to the other person on the phone signifying agreement. James was at Grey Owls on a scholarship for science. Each alternate year, Grey Owls took two students whose parents couldn't normally afford the fees, but who showed some academic promise. James had had a passion for the three sciences for as long as he could remember and winning a national competition designing a science magazine for children had paved the way for his acceptance at Grey Owls. Nominated by his junior school teacher, James had joined the school a week into the first term and Barrie, charged with showing James round, had hit it off with him straight away. As Barrie assembled two hydrogen atoms with an oxygen one to make the water they'd been studying that afternoon, James finally put the phone down and looked up, flushed.

"That was mum," he explained, running his hand through his short dark brown hair. "I think I'll be able to come, Dad's working a late shift, but she said she'll speak to him in the morning. We've a week at one of the camps booked for later in the holidays, so as long as I do well in the end of year exams Mum is happy that I spend a week or two with you. How did you get on?"

"Great," replied Barrie. "Dad said as long as it was ok with everyone's parents, you can all stay. He's worried that the place won't be finished and we may be on mattresses, but I think that'll be part of the fun."

"You bet!" exclaimed James, his eyes sparkling. "I can't wait till term is over and we're out, just the four of us, exploring and having adventures galore."

"You're getting as bad as Jenny," teased Barrie, smiling at his friend who, going red, stuck out his tongue in reply. "Did you read her last story?"

"Yes," replied James. "She's got such an imagination, you really feel like you're in the story. I bet she'll be a famous writer when she grows up, and we'll get signed books for birthdays, and they'll be turned into films and everything. Shall we sneak out and see how she's got on with her parents now?"

"Better not tonight," said Barrie shaking his head, "Thunder is on the prowl, I ran into him, quite literally, on my way to you." Thunder was their nickname for Mr Storm, who was renowned for having a temper much like a storm, rumbling away with the odd flash of lightning. "If he caught us going to the girls' dormitories, we'd be in detention 'til the end of term, and how rotten would that be?"

"I'll text her," said James, reaching for his phone, "We can't go to sleep not knowing, I'm so excited, I don't think I'll sleep anyway."

"Good idea," replied Barrie, "I'll text Liz." Both boys quickly typed messages to the girls and then sat, staring at their phones, willing them to reply. "What do they say, a watched pot never boils," sighed Barrie, putting a cushion over his phone, then staring fixedly at it.

After about 20 minutes, James's phone beeped. "Doomed, will tell you tomorrow," he read, from Jenny.

"Oh no!" exclaimed James, "Now I'll never sleep". Barrie looked worried, suddenly all his exciting plans thrown into doubt.

"Could we go without her do you think?" he asked, "Doesn't seem right somehow, I mean, I know we've only planned it today, but we have to get her to come, we just have to!"

"Hmm," sighed James, looking gloomy, "I agree. I guess we'll know more tomorrow and perhaps get our parents to talk to hers? She'd hate to miss out on all the adventure of exploring your place. We'll see her at breakfast and," James was cut off by a loud bell that rang out once as his ceiling light, which was on, flashed off and on twice, signalling that it was lights-out time in ten minutes. "Find out what's going on," finished James. "You'd better get going; you don't want to be caught out by Thunder after lights out." Lights out meant literally that. Power was shut down to all the power sockets, other than one by each bed and the main bedroom lights were switched off. That left only a soft glow from the corridor lights which shone through the window above each bedroom door, serving as an emergency light.

"Yes, I'll see you at breakfast – leave your phone on silent, I'll text you if Liz replies tonight." Barrie slipped quietly out of James's room and walked quickly back to his. When lights out came, both the boys' rooms were in darkness, as they each lay in their beds thinking already of the fun they could have if the four of them really could spend a week or two together.

The next day dawned bright and sunny. James and Barrie both quickly washed and dressed, and headed for the dining hall where their meals were served.

"There she is," pointed Barrie catching a glimpse of Jenny who was in the queue. Neither had heard from Jenny or Liz after lights out the previous night, and both were eager for news. "I only want some cereal, will that do you?"

"Fine by me," replied James, as they moved to bypass most of the queueing pupils, who were waiting for a hot breakfast of porridge or toast. "The porridge here is always lumpy and the toast cold – it's only good if it's buttered hot." Breakfast at

Grey Owls was the same daily except on Sundays when the pupils could choose, if they wished, a cooked breakfast consisting of bacon, sausage, egg, beans, hash browns, tomatoes and mushrooms. It was the highlight of James's week, who loved a hearty breakfast, yet never seemed to put on any weight. The boys each filled a bowl with cereal and slid onto chairs opposite Jenny who was looking gloomily into her bowl, listlessly stirring the flakes round in the ice cold milk.

"You look glum," said Barrie, "Will your parents not let you come?"

"Oh they'll let me come, no problem," replied Jenny, looking ever more downcast.

"Then what's up?" asked Barrie, his brow creasing with concern. Jenny was always cheery and it was worrying to see her upset. "Is it something else?"

"They've put a condition on me going," explained Jenny, "so in effect I'll not be able to go." The boys exchanged glances, wondering what condition could be so severe that Jenny would choose not to go rather than comply with it.

"Go on," prompted James, "what's so horrendous?"

"I've to get an A in science in the end of term exams. Dad saw my report and knows that I struggle with science. I'm ok at English and all those type of things, but there's just so much to remember in science, I'll never get an A, I'm on a C now, so you'll just have to go without me." A tear ran slowly down Jenny's cheek and she quickly wiped it away, embarrassed.

Barrie looked forlornly at Jenny. "Oh don't give up," he said, soothingly, "There must be something we can do."

"There is," exclaimed James, a grin spreading over his face. "I'll get you your A."

"How?" asked Jenny, "It's not like you can sit the exam for me."

"I'll teach you it," replied James, warming to the idea. "I devised loads of easy ways to remember stuff when I did the magazine; we'll go to the library every evening and just work through it all, beginning to end."

"They're only two weeks away," said Jenny looking doubtful, but not quite so down, "do you really think we can do it?

"I think we can yes," said James, "You'd be mad not to try, and it will help me refresh my memory by teaching it to you. We'll start tonight, yes?"

"That would be great," replied Jenny, her eyes full of hope. "Oh, wait, I'm on litter picking tonight. Drat!"

"I'll do that," chipped in Barrie. "I'll speak to Mr Merryweather at break and explain things, it'll be fine." Every student was required to spend a few hours, one evening a week, helping to keep the school and communal areas clean and tidy. It was said to serve two purposes according to the leaflet each parent received, instilling a sense of responsibility and discipline in the children and reducing the number of cleaners the school employed, thus reducing the fees the school charged.

"I can't ask you to do that, it's not fair."

"You're not asking me, I'm offering and it is fair. I want the four of us to be together and this is the best way I can help make that happen, so don't worry, leave it to me, you just go to the library with James and I'll do your chores till the end of the term." insisted Barrie

The three settled down to their breakfast and had almost finished when they heard sound of running feet. Liz appeared, red faced and flustered, scanning the room for sight of her friends. James stood and waved to her and she padded over, throwing herself down at their table. "My useless phone!" she panted, getting her breath. "I saw your message last night Bar, but couldn't reply. I tried for ages but it wouldn't send."

"No worries" replied Barrie, "How did you get on?"

"Mum and Dad said I can go if I do well in the exams," replied Liz, blowing wisps of hair from her eyes. "I should do ok, so will work hard, what about everyone else?" James filled Liz in on the events of the previous 12 hours, and their plans for ensuring Jenny could join them.

"So, we're held to ransom over exam results!" declared Jenny dramatically, "But we shall overcome the demanding parents and win the day! We shall be triumphant!"

"Proper warlike spirit, like the, oh what was it, we were only doing it last week?" added Barrie.

"Blitz," replied Liz, as the bell for registration rang out loudly. The four went off to their lessons and that evening Jenny and James spent their free time in the library working through the science topics. Mrs Fletcher, the teacher on duty that night, smiled to see the two working so hard and brought them both a cup of hot chocolate for being so studious. Barrie, true to his word, had spoken to Mr Merryweather, the caretaker who oversaw the rota for the students' chores. Mr Merryweather, impressed at the group pulling together had rewarded Barrie with a packet of biscuits from his secret store, normally reserved for children who were homesick, and Barrie, thanking him, pocketed them to share with the others the next day. The days flew by and Jenny and James worked tirelessly revising in the library. Barrie often sat with them, studying alongside and even Liz, joined in on the evenings when her mum had to work after school duties at Grey Owls.

Term ran on swiftly to its end. The exams came and went, with Jenny coming second in science in the whole year, second only to James. Barrie had pretended to warm his hands on her blushing face after the end of year assembly, where she'd been presented with a shield for the most improved science student. All the four had done well, with James receiving a certificate as recognition for all the time he'd spent helping Jenny. Plans were confirmed and the four children's parents had been in touch with each other by phone and email. Things were settled. Barrie's father would pick them all up on the Saturday in his large estate car and they had a glorious week to spend together at Pen Y Bryn exploring the farm and land around. This holiday promised to be a really exciting time..

Chapter Three

An Eventful Journey

Saturday morning dawned fine and bright and Grey Owls was alive with excited chattering as the boarders all waited for parents or guardians to collect them for the summer holidays. Cases were packed and rooms cleared and checked, promises to visit school friends over the holidays were made, and even the birds seemed to sing more loudly, as if they too were looking forward to eight weeks without lessons. The school minibus arrived at the front of school, driven by Mr Merryweather, and those children travelling home by train were counted into it, escorted by teachers who would see them safely onto their trains at the nearby station. A register was taken aboard the bus and away it pulled in a cloud of black smoke, accompanied by whoops and shouts of joy from those inside it.

Sitting with their cases at the front of school, Jenny, Barrie and James bathed in the morning sun, enjoying feeling the warmth of it on their faces.

"I do hope Dad's not going to be too long," said Barrie, looking at his watch for the umpteenth time that morning. "He was leaving he said at seven, so he should be here by eleven, that's only half an hour away."

"Liz has still to arrive yet," replied James, his eyes closed against the bright morning sun, "Has anyone heard from her today?" The others both shook their heads.

"Since her phone died, mine has been rather quiet," remarked Jenny, "but she said last night she would be here by ten. She seemed a bit quiet last night, I think it's a bit daunting for her. We're used to being away, but I don't think she has been away from home before." The three all fell quiet as they remembered how they had felt in September, away from home for the first time.

"She'll be all right," said Barrie, smiling. "Sarah is lovely, and we'll all be together, so she won't be on her own. Don't mention homesickness and I bet she won't miss it a bit."

"Yeah, we'll always stick together us four," added James. "Dad says teamwork is the key to success in life, and that too many people are out just for themselves, so we'll always stay as a team and it'll all be fine." James's father was a policeman and James would often come out with phrases or quotes that would make him seem very much older than his twelve years. He'd taught the others the phonetic alphabet that year and old police codes he'd grown up with, they'd spent a fun few days devising their own code system, which they used when passing notes in class, much to the annoyance of the few teachers who'd caught them.

"Here she is!" shouted Barrie, standing up as he saw Liz's mum's small blue car turn down the long drive to Grey Owls. "I was getting worried, I can't wait for dad to get here, it's going to be brilliant!" Mrs Green brought her car to a halt by the three children and Liz jumped out of the front seat.

"Hi guys!" she shouted, "I thought today would never get here. Wow, haven't you got a lot of stuff?" Liz dragged her small case out of the boot of the car and looking doubtfully at the other cases all lined up. "Will we all fit in your dad's car, Bar?"

"Of course we will," smiled Barrie. "We've a whole term's worth of clothes and stuff don't forget, but don't worry, Dad's car is huge"

"Good morning you three," smiled Mrs Green, "Are you looking forward to your big adventure?" Mrs Green was one of the best teachers at Grey Owls in the opinion of the four, her lessons always seemed to fly by, whereas the hour and ten minutes they spent in geography with Mr Semple always felt like an eternity.

"Yes thanks," chorused Barrie, James and Jenny, with Jenny adding;

"It will make the essay we will be given in September about what we did in the holidays more interesting. We're bound to be set one, and I can write about our wild adventures, shooting the rapids, being swept away and having to fend for ourselves, lost in the wilderness with nothing but wild animals for company as we track our way back home, like intrepid explorers."

Mrs Green looked a bit worried at this, but knowing Jenny for her creative writing and fantastic imagination smiled and said, "You make North Wales sound like the rocky mountains of America, I'm sure you'll have a lovely time, just don't be disappointed if there are not wild bears round every turn."

Mrs Green said she'd wait with the children for Barrie's Dad and soon there was a squeal of excitement from Barrie as he jumped up pointing down the drive as a large dark red estate car drove slowly down the tree lined drive towards them "He's here, Dad's here!"

Barrie's dad pulled up in the large car and he got out, stretching. Barrie threw himself on his father and hugged him tight. The two had always been close since the death of Barrie's mother, and Barrie had missed his father terribly while at school. "I thought you'd never get here Dad!" exclaimed Barrie.

Mr Williams, fondling his son's curly mop of hair, laughed. It was an easy, natural laugh and the other three children immediately liked him. He had sandy coloured hair with flecks of grey at the temples, and the same sparking blue eyes as Barrie. Dressed in a checked shirt and jeans, they quickly formed the impression he would be good fun to be around. Looking up from his son, he said "It's not even eleven o'clock yet, I made good time. Hello you lot, you're all ready I see," before smiling at Mrs Green and holding out his hand, "Alan, pleased to meet you."

"Susan," replied Mrs Green. "Thank you so much for having them all to stay, as I said on the phone, it's amazing how much they've all put in during these last few weeks to all be allowed to go, I think you'll be their hero for life."

"It's my pleasure," replied Barrie's dad, smiling broadly, "As you know it's not exactly the Ritz, but they'll be safe and well fed. Sarah is already starting on the roast for tonight to welcome them. They've all worked hard like you say, so it's nice for them to have a week together as a reward, and I'd much rather have kids outside in the fresh air than huddled around a computer screen all day long."

"Absolutely," agreed Susan. "The place sounds so wonderful that I'm quite envious of the four, fresh air and roast dinners, sounds perfection to me."

"Well we're looking perhaps at converting a barn to take in bed and breakfast guests, in the next year or two, so you and your family would be most welcome."

Barrie, thinking the conversation had gone on long enough, left the parents talking, went to the boot of the car and opened it. The four all wheeled or carried their cases over to it and Barrie helped them lift them all in and pack them tight so they all fitted, just.

"All set Dad," he called, turning to the other three. "Come on, let's all get in and we can get going." Jenny and James got into the back of the car and Barrie opened the front passenger door, only Liz held back, going over to her mother to give her a last hug.

"I'll let you know when we get there mum, love you," she said, suddenly feeling dreadfully homesick and half not wanting to go.

"Hey, you'll have a great time," reassured her mum, sensing her reluctance. "I'll see you next week and here, share these on the journey." Reaching into her car, Mrs Green brought out several packets of sweets and bottles of soft drinks. "Mind, I didn't know a roast would be waiting for you, so don't eat too many."

"Thanks mum," said Liz, passing the drinks and sweets into the car, and climbing in after them.

Alan got in the driver's seat and, with shouts and waves and yells, they were off, off to the land of dragons, where an old farm, rugged mountains and meandering rivers awaited them.

The four could hardly believe it, they were finally on their way, after two long weeks of hard study, endless reassurances and promises to their parents, it had all worked out perfectly. The three in the back settled down and it wasn't long before the packets of treats were handed round and the chatter went quiet as everyone was busy sucking on their sweets of choice.

"Your mum is a star," said James to Liz, as he selected a humbug from a bag of hard boiled sweets, "Yorkshire Mixture is my favourite; it's as if she knew."

"She did," replied Liz. "Every time she was on tuck shop duty, that is what you bought. Barry went for chocolate covered raisins, Jenny, pear drops, and I fizzy cola bottles, so she got a bag of each for us for the holidays. What's more, she and dad have given me my birthday present early, and let me bring it here."

"What is it?" asked James, popping the striped sweet into his mouth.

"A new phone," said Liz, smiling. "It's my birthday in two weeks and I'd asked for a new one. Mine was dad's old one and, well, you know how full and slow it was. This one has a super camera on the back and Mum said I could have it early so that I could take some photos of the scenery and stuff. I've packed it in my bag, can you please help me transfer all the things I want to keep from my old phone onto it?"

James nodded, unable to answer with the boiled sweet in his mouth.

The car seemed to eat up the miles, and after two hours they entered North Wales. The road signs had Welsh and English writing, and Barrie laughed as his friends tried to pronounce the new words. They stopped not far into Wales for a break and to have lunch as it was almost another two hours to Pen Y Bryn. Sarah had sent a pack up of sandwiches for them all, and they sat in a picnic area in the sun enjoying their feast and stretching their legs before they all piled back into the car again and continued on.

The roads soon began to narrow, and the car had to work hard to climb the hills they found themselves among. Ahead of them rose mountains, far higher than any the three had ever seen before and Barrie smiled proudly and reeled off the names of them all.

"Not far now," said Barrie's dad, who'd insisted to the other three that they call him Alan. "Mr Williams is so formal," he'd said, "you are all part of our family for a week." The three had all developed a strong liking for him, and one by one closed their eyes. Alan smiled as he saw them all, in his rear view mirror, asleep on each other. "I imagine it's been a pretty exhausting time," he said to Barrie, "getting ready for the exams, the end of year excitement, and packing for here, not to mention all the extras you and James have done helping Jenny. We'll have a good dinner, get you all settled in and you can all have an early night. No point in you tiring yourselves further today and not being fresh for exploring tomorrow."

"Thanks, Dad," said Barrie, closing his eyes, "and thanks for letting them come, you've no idea how much it means to me."

After half an hour Barrie's dad shook his son awake. "We're about five minutes away," he said, "do you want to wake the others so you can show them the road up as we go? We'll pass the turning to Nain's new home, and the main entrance to Tylluan Hall, be good to show them their bearings." Barrie leaned through the gap between the seats and tapped James' knee, waking him.

"Nearly there, do you want to wake the girls and I'll show you a few places as we go up the mountain?"

Soon they were all looking out of the car windows as Barrie and his dad provided a running commentary. The road was narrow and two cars would have to pass slowly to be sure of not hitting each other's wing mirrors. To the left of the road down a sharp decline ran a river,

"That's the same river that comes through Pen Y Bryn," said Barrie, "Do you remember it?" The others could, for in the last two weeks they'd poured over aerial images of the area and knew it like a map. The car reached a junction with a road on its left crossing the river and heading up the mountain the other side of it.

"Bar's nain now lives just along there," said Alan, slowing the car so the children could see. "You can just see the corner of her barn, she's looking forward to meeting you all and has been busy baking lots of treats."

The children grinned. They were not going to go hungry this week and would certainly be paying a visit to Bar's nain. The car continued on straight ahead, curving away from the river as the road continued to rise. After about a mile Alan spoke again, "We're just about to come to Tylluan Hall," he said to the children. "I," Alan broke off, looking in his rear view mirror behind him and pulled his car sharply onto the narrow verge on the left of the road. The manoeuvre jolted the children and they exclaimed in panic as three big police cars, their lights flashing, passed quickly by the car, disappearing out of sight around a bend ahead.

"Sorry kids," said Alan, pulling his car back onto the road, "they came up behind pretty quickly, everyone ok?" They were and continued on, everyone now sat bolt upright, alert and more than a little excited at the sight of the police cars. Rounding a corner, they were all surprised to see the three police cars, still with their lights flashing, now blocking the road completely, and a blue van in amongst them. Two of the police cars were in front of the van, which was facing down the road, towards the children, and one of the cars had squeezed past and was now behind the van, stopping it from going backwards. Alan brought the car to a stop and the children all stared, captivated as a swarm of police officers, all dressed in black and looking very tough, emerged from the vehicles, and went to the blue van. Three men inside the blue van got out and were gestured at to go and stand by the wall next to the entrance to Tylluan Hall. One of the officers, a sergeant, then turned, and approached Alan's car.

"Sorry, Mr Williams," said the officer, talking through the open driver's window. "We had another call today that more silver has been discovered to be missing, so shot up here before they knocked off for the day. Need to search these three and the van, we'll just get everyone secure and will move into the driveway so you can get past, just give us a few minutes if you can."

"No problem," said Alan, who clearly knew something of what was going on, "I'm not in a rush, Jake doesn't look too put out either." The children followed Alan's gaze to the three men, who, leaning against the wall grinned and shrugged.

"Third time!" the man who'd been driving the van shouted over to Alan, as a young policeman patted his pockets. "Good job it is quiet round here or people would talk."

"Won't keep you long Jake," shouted back the sergeant. "You and the lads will be in the pub by six. But we have to do something."

"I know, no bother," shouted back Jake, walking over to the officer still stood by the driver's window. "Trust me, we're as keen as you are to find out what's happening here. No good spending months and months restoring the place if it's empty when it opens. There's nothing in the van that shouldn't be, there wasn't the last two times and there never will be, but you search it if it makes you happy, you have a job to do."

"Thanks, Jake," replied the sergeant, "I'll just get these vehicles shifted out of Mr Williams' way, we'll check inside them and you can go." He moved off and began shouting instructions for the vehicles to be moved down the long driveway.

"Gosh, you've a car full!" exclaimed Jake to Alan, looking in through the driver's door. "Must be the summer holidays, I didn't know you had so many kids."

"I don't," explained Alan. "This is Barrie, my son. His friends in the back have come to stay for a week."

"Great stuff," replied Jake, "Is Sarah going to bring them to the Hall? Show them round before it opens to the public? They'd love that, I'm sure."

"Yes," said Alan, "I think she has something arranged. Say, you must have the patience of a saint, being searched three times and still finding a smile. I don't know if I would be as calm."

"Well, they have a job to do," shrugged Jake, in his strong welsh accent, "We are just as keen as they are to find out what's gone on. For all they know the stuff could have been taken years ago, when the crates were packed away, who knows, but there's no point in getting stressed about it, just go with the flow as they say." A shout made both men look up. A policeman was waving at them to show the road was now clear for Alan to continue. "Well, have a great week, kids," said Jake, leaning down into the car and smiling at the four. "If Sarah brings you to the hall, come and find me, I'll show you the work that we have done, bits that the public won't see."

"Thanks," replied the children, and Jake crossed the road back to the drive to the hall.

"What's been going on, Dad?" asked Barrie. "What was that about?"

"I'll tell you all over dinner," replied his father. "Let's get you home and unpacked."

The children all exchanged excited glances. Police road blocks, vehicle raids, a mystery at Tully Hall, they'd barely arrived and already it felt like an adventure. Certainly, this week would not be boring.

Chapter Four

Pen Y Bryn

A mile further up the road, grey stone buildings loomed up on the left hand side. The stone wall, which bounded the fields on the left of the road, was punctuated by a pair of large stone gate posts, from one of which hung an old broken gate. The big car swung through the gateway into a large cobbled farmyard and Barrie proudly announced "Pen Y Bryn! Welcome everyone!"

The children looked and exclaimed in delight. What a lovely place! To the left as they'd entered the yard was a large stone building, with huge old barn doors in the middle, below an impressive archway. Ahead of them was a single storey barn, the byre Barrie had called it, which had stable type doors looking into the yard and to the right was the farm house, again, made of grey stone. The children instantly felt a welcome air about them, as if the farm was as eager to have them there as they were to be there. James inhaled deeply, "Oh Bar!" he marvelled "It's fantastic, just smell that!" the others laughed at him. James, fond of the countryside had often talked about the smell of the land and stood, quite lost in the moment, breathing in the fresh country air.

"Welcome!" called a voice and, turning, the children saw that the farmhouse door had opened and, in its frame, her hands covered in flour, stood a slim, pretty lady, whose blonde shoulder length hair was tied back in a ponytail. Barrie immediately rushed over to her,

"Sarah!" he cried happily, and launched himself on her. Sarah opened her arms and embraced the boy, spreading flour first down his back, then in his curly fair hair as she ruffled it affectionately. The other three children hung back, Barrie, releasing Sarah from his bear hug, turned back to them, "This is Sarah." Broad smiles covered the faces of the three as they went to shake hands with Sarah, who laughing, dusted each of them with a sprinkling of flour as they shook hands. "Welcome," she smiled warmly, "I was just doing some baking."

"Sarah's baking is fabulous," grinned Barrie, and the three, who'd enjoyed her scones and brownies she'd packed Barrie off to school with after Christmas and Easter holidays, nodded their agreement

"Pleased to meet you Mrs Williams," replied James, "and thank you for having us all to stay, we're here to muck in and help out."

"It's Sarah, please," replied Sarah, "I'm sure you'll soon be in the thick of everything here. Come on in and have a rest. I expect you're tired after such a long journey, let me get you all something to drink." The children all trooped in through the front door into the big, warm farmhouse kitchen.

"Oh look at the view!" exclaimed Jenny, who'd spent the last few minutes staring round in disbelief at the place, and now crossed the kitchen to look out of the large window looking towards the head of the valley. "I wish I could paint, it's fabulous. I could set a story here."

"Jen's a bit of a writer," explained Barrie to Sarah, as his Dad bustled in carrying two suitcases. "She writes amazing stories, really like you're in them. One day, she's going to be a famous writer and we're going to go to her book signings."

Jenny, looking embarrassed smiled and blushed. "I'm not that good, I just like writing."

"I will look forward to reading Katie some of your work then," said Sarah, smiling and nodding towards a chair in the corner, where a baby slept peacefully. "Come and sit down, I'll just get these in the oven and get you all something cool to drink, or would you prefer tea?" The four children flopped into chairs round the large kitchen table, the excitement of the journey quite forgotten as a pleasant tiredness flowed over them. Barrie's dad returned with the last of the suitcases and, setting them down, ruffled his son's hair. "Welcome home, Bar," he said. "I'll take the cases up into the bedrooms, if you tell me which case belongs to each of you. Sarah's made up a room for Jen and Liz, and there's a bunk bed in your room Bar, for you and James. I'm afraid we're all still living a bit out of boxes, but I'm sure we'll manage." The children, quite revived by the cool juice Sarah had given them, all jumped up, eager to explore their bedrooms for the next week. Barrie's room was the one he'd always slept in when visiting his nain, with views over the farmyard and down the valley towards Tylluan Hall. The bedroom the girls would share was directly behind, facing up towards the head of the valley.

Jenny immediately ran to the window, "Look at the mountains from up here, this place is just magical! Cornwall is beautiful, and I love it there, but oh, this is so, so, rugged." Liz crossed the room and agreed with her. Yorkshire, Liz had said was stunning with the Dales and the Moors, but somehow the Welsh mountains held a majesty all of their own.

"Which bed would you like?" asked Liz, who'd gone back to her case Barrie's dad had left in the doorway.

"I don't mind at all, I'm just so happy to be here," replied Jenny, and the two girls set to work, unpacking their cases. There were two beds and a small chest of drawers and they'd nearly got everything tidied away when Barrie appeared in the open doorway.

"Are you ready?" he asked, "I thought we could explore round the yard before dinner."

"You bet!" chorused the girls, and they all raced down the stairs to where James waited at the bottom. Sarah, hearing their footfall on the wooden stairs, appeared at the kitchen door.

"Are you off exploring already?" she asked, adding, "You've got about an hour until dinner, so don't go too far. I'll call you when it's ready." The four, grinning widely, raced off across the yard and soon disappeared from view behind the barn. The valley fell away in front of them, curving round the hillside as the four stood, feeling very small in comparison, looking all around them. Barrie explained where the farmland extended to, and pointed out the stream that was visible from the girls' bedroom.

"So that's the same one that passes your nain's?" asked Liz, "I remember seeing it on the satellite picture, but somehow, you just don't get a feel for the ups and the downs do you?" The three fell about laughing and agreed that, no, you don't get a feel for the ups and the downs. Liz gave James a friendly shove and the four set off heading up the valley, beyond the farmhouse to the top meadow as Barrie called it. The land fell away steeply towards the stream at the bottom, and, as James commented, it seemed that the only flat ground around the farm was the farmyard itself, and the garden area which surrounded the other three sides of the farmhouse.

"Yes," replied Barrie, "most of the land is on the sides of the mountains. The land around Tylluan Hall is flatter, but whether that's because they moved the earth when it was built, or if it was always flat, I don't know. We can ask Sarah if you like, she's been working there, so might know more about it."

"Yes, we must," said James, "and we need to ask them what's going on at Tully Hall with the police cars and all the searching. Your dad seemed to know something about it Bar."

"Gosh yes! You know, in all the excitement of getting here and showing you round, I'd quite forgotten about that. Dad or Sarah must know what's going on, we can ask them over tea."

A loud clanging noise suddenly sounded from the farmyard.

"Great, dinner is ready. Come on, we'll go and wash." They all ran back to the house and were soon panting in the farmyard as they pulled off their boots and went to wash their hands. Delicious smells wafted from the kitchen and the four inhaled deeply as they took their places at the table.

"This looks wonderful," said James, his eyes falling on dishes and bowls of steaming hot vegetables, plates of meat and warm crusty bread, "thank you very much, you shouldn't have gone to so much trouble."

"It's no trouble at all," smiled Sarah, "I expect you are hungry and tired after your long journey, and so a good meal will set you up for the week ahead. I imagine Bar will have you going up and down the hillside, so there will be a hot cooked meal for you every evening, and we'll have cold food at lunchtime. Now, shall I serve you all?"

They were all soon tucking in heartily to the tasty meal, and Barrie's dad, keen to make all the children feel welcome, asked lots of questions about where they were from and how they found school. Once the conversation waned, Barrie turned the talk to Tylluan Hall.

"What's happened at the Hall, Dad? That man seemed to know you well. What are the police doing there?"

"Well, Sarah will be able to explain better than me, as you know, she's been working there on the restoration."

Four pairs of eyes turned, expectantly, to Sarah, who began, "Tylluan Hall has been open to the public for many years, but two years ago, after a huge funding campaign, it closed for some much needed restoration. The building was falling to bits here and there you know, the roof leaked, the paint was peeling, it really was in a sorry state, so everything was carefully packaged up and stored in a few rooms, while the rest of the building was restored. The paintings were wrapped up and stored in dry crates, the furniture was all moved, some was sent for restoration and I've been restoring the smaller bits at the Hall. All the pottery and porcelain was carefully wrapped and packaged away, as was the silver. There had been a fabulous, and quite famous, collection of Georgian silver at the Hall. Experts and enthusiasts from all over the world would come and admire it, and it was all carefully cleaned and wrapped up, so it would not tarnish while in storage." Sarah paused, to enjoy a mouthful of her dinner and the four waited patiently for her to continue. "As the restoration is nearing completion, many of the items from storage are now being brought out, ready to be put on display again. Any items that had been restored while the building itself was being repaired were in a different area, but most of the pottery, porcelain sculptures and silver didn't need restoring and so has been packed in dozens of tea chests for the past two years."

"So why does that involve the police?" interrupted Barrie.

"Well, I'm getting to that bit," continued Sarah. "When boxes of silver have been opened and unpackaged, many small items have been found to be missing. Each piece was catalogued in an inventory, a list, when it was packed away, so it's worrying as to where they have gone."

"Have there been any break-ins while the hall has been closed?" asked James, impressing the others with his question. "Could the items have been taken in a burglary?"
"None that anyone has noticed," replied Sarah. "The building has an alarm; the insurance company had insisted on that, it has been set every night and has not been triggered once. Few people have been in the room with the silver apart from the builders you saw stopped today, as they were repairing the plasterwork and repainting it."
"The man talking to Dad said it probably happened when the silver was packed away, so who did that, and have they been questioned?" said Barrie, his brow furrowed as he puzzled

over the mystery. Jenny and Liz nodded in agreement with his thoughts. Alan laughed,

"Well you're a fine lot aren't you? Barely here five minutes and already you're going to do the police's work for them."

"Good question," replied Sarah "The person who'd packed them away after they were cleaned and catalogued was old Dai Evans. Worked there for years after he retired from farming he did, and was as honest as the day is long."

"What does he say about the silver?" asked Barrie.

"Nothing" replied Sarah. "Sadly Dai passed away last winter, so there is no way of knowing what he could have said. I can't believe he would have known or been involved with anything underhand though, he was a lovely, old-fashioned man. But, that said, Jake the builder and his team are lovely too. I can't think of anyone I'd point a finger at to be honest. I think the police are clutching at straws as they feel that they have to do something, but I don't think we'll ever see those pieces of silver again. They were worth a fortune."

"They'll have been sold on the black market," chipped in James, "Dad's told me all about how stolen goods are passed around, with no questions asked as everyone knows they are stolen and so they are sold for a lower price. It's really wicked, will the insurance pay?"

"I think it will pay so much, but the loss of the collection is heart breaking. Some of the pieces had been crafted for the old owners of the Hall, and had their family crest embossed on them. No amount of money can replace such a thing, it's just so sad."

"Hmm," mused James, "I'll ask Dad tonight what he thinks. He'll have some clever ideas, I know he will. If anyone can solve this, he can."

"I'm just amazed at how calm Jake and his lads are with getting stopped all the time," said Alan, "I don't think I would be as understanding in their position. I can understand them being stopped once, but it's now been three times and still they have a smile on their faces. Tylluan Hall is lucky to have such a team."

"Hmm. What if they're smiling because they are the thieves, but the police just aren't smart enough?" put in Liz, who'd looked deep in thought for some time. "Don't people return to the scene of their crime?"

Sarah laughed, "Sometimes, yes, they do," she said, "but I don't think there's anything to worry about with Jake and his team, they're always smiling and so helpful."

"He did seem nice," added Barrie smiling in delight as Sarah set down a large dish of pudding.

"Apple crumble," she announced, "and ice cream, cream or custard. Help yourselves." The four needed no encouragement and soon all could be heard was the sound of contented eating as the children and adults all enjoyed the end of the meal.

After helping to clear away and load the dishwasher, the children all began yawning.

"Bless you, you must be worn out after your long day. Why don't you all have an early night so you are fresh in the morning." The children agreed and, thanking Sarah again for the meal, they trooped upstairs and got ready for bed.

Jenny and Liz were tucked up in their beds when there was a soft knock at the door and James's head popped round, "Hey you two", he whispered, entering the room with Barrie tiptoeing softly behind him. "What do you think of Tully Hall then? That's a proper mystery isn't it? Bar and I reckon we should have a go at solving it while we're here, what do you think?"

"Oh yes, definitely," said Jenny, her bright eyes shining in the dim light.

"Count me in," added Liz, "We've been having similar thoughts. What with the farm to explore, and the mystery to solve, we will be busy!" The children heard footfalls on the stairs and the boys slipped quietly back to their bedroom. Soon all the children were snuggled in their beds, and fell asleep thinking of mountains and valleys, mysterious goings on, and lost silver.

Chapter Five

Settling In

The next morning began fine and dry, the birds were singing loudly and the children felt refreshed after their long trip the day before.

Barrie woke first and went to tap on the girls' door.

"Are you awake in there?" he called gently, continuing to tap. "It's a glorious day, James and I are up, breakfast in ten minutes."

"Morning," replied Liz, "Mmmm, breakfast. I am hungry, although goodness knows why after all we ate last night."

"It's the mountain air," called back Barrie. "Are you decent?"

"Yes, come in, Jen's just waking."

Barrie poked his head round the door and grinned at the two girls, still snuggled in their beds.

"What sleepyheads you are. Good job we're not at school or you'd be ever so late for lessons. Sarah and Dad are already downstairs, I've been down and there are some super smells coming from the kitchen."

The four all dressed and went downstairs into the warm farmhouse kitchen.

"Morning, come and sit down," beckoned Sarah, "Did you all sleep well?"

The children, taking their places at the large table, all thanked Sarah, replying that they had slept well.

"I had the most fantastic dream!" enthused Jenny. "We solved the mystery of Tully Hall, we were on the TV and everything, really famous!"

"That's great," laughed Sarah, "Who is the thief and where is the all the silver?"

"I don't know," replied Jenny, frustration etched on her face. "I know we caught the thief, but each time I try and picture them, I just can't, it's like I'm seeing them through a frosted window. Try as hard as I can and still it won't come."

"Oh well, dreams are like that," replied Sarah, bringing a large plate out of the aga piled high with bacon, sausages, mushrooms and tomatoes. "Help yourselves," she said, turning back, "I've eggs just about ready and there's toast almost done. Bar, perhaps you can get that please?" Barrie got up, and crossed to the toaster as his father entered, carrying little Katie, who he set down in a crib in the corner.

"She's asleep now," he said, walking over to the table. "I hope she didn't wake you in the night. We're in the furthest room away from you but she did cry a bit."

"Oh, we never heard a thing, Sir," said James, who like as not wouldn't have said anything even if Katie had screamed the house down all night long.

"Alan, please, you're not at school now, you're here to enjoy yourselves. Besides, 'Sir', reminds me of the headmaster at my old school." Alan shuddered vigorously. "The cane was still in use at that time, and we lived in fear of him all right."

"The cane?" asked Liz.

"And the belt," added Alan. Corporal punishment it's called. It's all illegal of course nowadays, but kept us in line I can tell you."

"I bet old Thunder would bring that back if he could," said Barrie, setting down a plate with toast and sliding into his chair. "I don't think he could be happy if he tried. I've never known anyone look so stern, it's frightening."

39

"I'm sure he's not that bad," laughed Sarah, putting an egg onto each person's plate before sitting down. "Come on, get stuck in, I bet you're hungry. Don't stand on ceremony, it'll go cold."

The four all tucked in, as did the grownups and the only sound in the kitchen was that of everyone munching. It really was a very good breakfast. Soon everyone was sat back in their chairs, 'full to bursting' as Liz had said, washing their breakfast down with mugs of hot, sweet tea.

"I thought you would probably enjoy spending the morning exploring," said Alan, "Nain is coming for lunch. She's very much looking forward to seeing you, Bar, so it would be nice for you to all perhaps spend the afternoon with her, and we can have a BBQ for tea out on the lawn. How does that sound?"

"Oh Dad, that sounds really great," replied Barrie, "I've missed Nain like mad, so of course we will spend the afternoon with her. You'll love her," he added, beaming at his three friends.

"Get yourselves out in the fresh air for the morning then," said Alan, "Don't worry about the dishes, I'll clear them away this morning, go and explore. Be careful mind, stay around the farmland and have your phone with you. Lunch will be at half past twelve, so listen out for the bell."

The four all put boots on and headed out into the warm July sunshine, with Barrie suggesting that they go to the top most part of the land and then work their way back.

"I don't know if I can climb much after all that breakfast!" explained Jenny, patting her tummy and sticking it out. "It's a good job we won't have that every day, I'd be the size of a house before I knew it!"

"That would be ok," teased James, "We could just then roll you down the hillside to the bottom." Jenny gave James a playful shove and the four headed off towards the head of the valley.

"We'll go and sit on Wolf's Rock." said Barrie, "The view from there is just amazing, and it's right at the top of our land, furthest up."

"Why's it called Wolf's Rock?" asked Liz, looking a little apprehensive, "You don't have wolves round it do you?"

"No, silly," said Barrie, "it's just the name I gave it, as it's a huge piece of flat grey slate that sticks out of the mountainside. Just the place that the head of a wolf pack would stand to survey his territory, that's all, you can just see it, look." The others looked where Barrie pointed and, against the sky, they could make out the dark projection from the side of the mountain. Up and up they walked, panting with the effort of the steep incline. No one spoke as they used their breath for pumping their legs hard to make the climb.

After what seemed like a mile long hike, which ended in quite a scramble, needing hands as well as feet to reach the top, the four arrived at 'Wolf's Rock' and all exclaimed at the view they gained.

"I can see exactly why you named it so," said James, using his hand to shield his eyes from the morning sun as he looked around the landscape as the mountain and valley fell away beneath them. "You can see for miles, the farm, Tully Hall, you can see it all."

"Yes," replied Barrie, coming to stand beside James, "And if you follow the stream as it becomes a small river, you can just make out a grey roof on the lower slopes of the opposite hillside to the one the farm is on. Can you see it? It's way beyond Tylluan Hall, on the opposite bank."

"Yes, I have it," said Liz, who had keen sharp eyes. "What is it?"

"That's the barn we passed yesterday, the one Nain now lives in."

"Oh gosh, fancy being able to see all that way," said James, "I can see it now, seemed a lot further away by car."

"Yes, the mountain road winds around a lot more than the river does in the valley bottom," said Barrie, "You can see just how big Tylluan Hall is now though, and the large lake in the grounds between the Hall and the river. They've been tidying up all the grounds since I was last up, it's going to look grand when it's open."

The four gazed at Tylluan Hall and soon were talking about the excitement of the day before.

"Wouldn't it be fantastic if we could solve the mystery," said Jen, who was keen for an adventure she could then write about.

"I can't see much chance of that happening," chipped in Liz, "If the police have been trying for ages..." she tailed off, under the disapproving looks from the others.

"I think we could have a go, especially if your step-mum does take us round the place," said James. "We think differently to grownups, and regardless of age, a fresh few pairs of eyes just might turn something up, there's no harm and it will be fun."

They all agreed that, while they wouldn't spend all their time looking into the mystery, they would take what opportunities they could to do a bit of investigating.

"We could be a lookout from here," continued James, "I wish I had some binoculars here, they would be handy."

"They'd need to be pretty strong to see a tiny piece of silver all that way away," scoffed Barrie, "and have x ray qualities if it's in someone's pocket."

"I'm not thinking of spotting the silver," retorted James. "It's about looking for people who are in places they shouldn't be, or acting strangely. Dad told me once, often people who commit crime return to the scene, so they could still be around. Shall I speak to him about this do you think?"

The three considered. "I don't think you should," said Jenny, "The last thing you want him to do is worry about us."

"Yes," added Barrie, "and what if he stopped us from any detective work, and spoke to my dad? Better off we keep this to ourselves, we're only keeping our eyes out, it's not like it's dangerous."

"Ok, good points," conceded James. "We will be detectives in secret, undercover." Jenny immediately rattled off the beginning of a plot line as if she was reading it from a book.

"I don't know how you do it," said Liz in admiration.

The four lay back on the flat rock, each taking off a jumper or coat to use as a pillow. The sun had warmed it nicely and there was only the lightest of breezes to tickle the children.

"I wonder why the police are always after the builders?" mused Barrie, his eyes shut against the morning sun. "It really must be so frustrating for them."

"For who, the police or the builders?" asked Liz. "Jake seemed pretty good natured yesterday, and the sergeant didn't look too bothered by it either."

"They won't be able to keep searching them for much longer," added James. "It'll be harassment and the builders will be complaining."

43

"Harassment?" asked Liz, and James explained to them, as best as he could, what he remembered from his Dad teaching him about his work.

"It makes sense," said Barrie, and the others agreed. "You can't just keep on at someone if they've done nothing wrong." As he spoke he lifted himself up on one arm, and gazed down towards Tylluan Hall. "I'll ask Dad if he has any binoculars, we can use them for keeping an eye out, and for bird watching too. There are some red kites near about and they're always impressive to see."

It really was a perfect morning, the sun, not too hot, warmed the children and they dozed, and explored the area round Wolf's Rock. The land around was very rocky, with grass growing in sparse tufts in between great slabs of slate.

"It really is like the mountains have been chiselled," said Jenny, her vivid imagination already conjuring up stories of giant hammers and chisels being used by an unseen hand, carving out valleys and shaping the rugged hillsides.

"Heavens to Betsy!" exclaimed Liz, using her favourite phrase she'd picked up during the previous term. "Have you seen the time? It's half past eleven already, and we've to get back for lunch by midday wasn't it?"

"Yes," replied Barrie. "It won't take us as long as it did to climb up, but we'll set off so we are not rushing on the steep parts. Come on, we'll head down now."

They all donned their jumpers and started back towards the farm. The descent was more tricky than they had imagined and Liz, Jenny and James all slipped a number of times on the steepest parts. Knees were bashed and bruised, but no one complained. It was the holidays, and ahead stretched the whole week of fun and exploring, along with a little mystery solving, which was still on everyone's mind.

As the four neared the farm, a black and white collie dog raced up the slope to great them.

"Hello Dash, old girl. How are you?" said Barrie, dropping on his knees and putting his arms around the big dog's neck. Dash was clearly very pleased to see Barrie and covered him in licks. The other three all made a fuss of the dog.

"Who does she belong to?" asked James.

"She's my nain's," replied Bar, "Dash used to be their working sheepdog when she and Taid, my grandad, had sheep, and a faster dog you never did see. Saved sheep which had strayed in the snow many a time, she is grand, though an old girl now. She means Nain is here, come and meet her."

The four all ran the last part with Dash barking excitedly round them. Out of breath, they arrived at the farm panting and saw, sat in the sun, a grey haired lady smiling across at them. She stood as they crossed towards her and opened her arms as Barrie gave her a bear hug.

"Bar, cariad bach!" she exclaimed, her blue eyes bright as she hugged Barrie back. "How lovely it is to see you. How are you? You must tell me all about school and how you have got on."

They all went into the garden where Sarah and Katie were sat in the shade of an ancient gnarled oak tree. Barrie went to help his father bring out trays of cold food for lunch and they all enjoyed a picnic in the sunshine.

"This really is what the summer hols are all about!" declared Liz, as she enjoyed fresh ham sandwiches, washed down with ice cold milk. "Eating outside, and exploring in the sunshine, it's just perfect, I haven't thought of school once!" Everyone agreed and ate heartily, as Barrie told his nain all about life at Grey Owls during the summer term. The other's joined in enthusiastically and the old lady insisted they called her Nain, saying how lucky she felt to have three extra grandchildren for the week. Nain listened intently to their tales. When Barrie recounted how James had helped Jenny to pass her science exam, Nain looked at him with admiration. "What a credit to your generation you are, James." she said, warmly, smiling as James, turning red, tried desperately to turn the attention away from himself.

"It was nothing really," he replied. "Bar did more than his fair share of chores so that Jen and I could study, so it was a team effort you see."

"Your great great great grandfather would be so proud of you Bar, and of all of you." The three looked at her, puzzled. "It was he who founded Grey Owls," explained Nain. "He found himself in Yorkshire, and had made quite a lot of money setting up a mill there, so decided to repay the area in a way, by building them a school. The name Grey Owls, was in part a nod to Tylluan Hall here. Tylluan is welsh for owl, you see and has been linked to our family since it was built. He was a philanthropist, and would approve of how you have all worked hard, as one to make sure you could enjoy this week together."

"What's a philanthropist?" asked Jenny, who loved new words and hadn't heard that one before.

"It's someone who spends either their time or money helping those in need. A good, kind-hearted person," replied Nain.

"How has your family been linked to the Hall?" asked James, and the four settled down as Nain recounted the family history.

"We've never lived at the Hall, but always here, at Pen Y Bryn and other farms about. Members of our family helped to build the Hall, way back, and shape the grounds, carving out the huge lake in the spring line. This farm used to serve the Hall when there was a family in residence there, and my mother and I both worked at the Hall until the family left and the place was given over to the Trust. I was ever so sad to see it looking all shabby and unloved. The upkeep had been too much for the family, and so much needed repairing that it's been in a sorry state for a long while. I am so excited to be finally seeing it restored to its former glory and look forward to going round it when it's completed."

"Are there any secret passages?" asked Jenny, her imagination already running away with her. Nain considered. "There are the servants' passages, which link some rooms. It wasn't the done thing for servants to be seen in those days," Nain explained, "So, where possible, there were different routes and stairs for them to use."

"How exciting," said Jenny, "I can't wait to see them!"

"You won't have long to wait," called Sarah, from her shady spot, "I thought I would take you there on Wednesday if you would like?"

"Yes please!" chorused the children, already imagining themselves solving the mystery and finding the silver.

The week certainly would not be dull, the children thought.

Chapter Six

Nain's Cottage

The following morning all four children piled into Alan's car and headed back down the hillside towards Barrie's nain's home.

"Tully Hall is so majestic," said Jenny as it came into view. "I can't wait to have a look round it. You are so lucky Bar, living with all this on your doorstep." The children all looked at it, its castellated top somehow giving it rather a sinister appearance.

The car continued on, passing Tylluan Hall and curving round the mountainside where the children, gazing out of the right side of the car, caught glimpses of the river as it meandered down the valley.

"That runs right past the bottom of Nain's spot," said Barrie. "It's nice that it connects the farm and her barn."

"Yes," added his father, "we turned the area between the barn and the river into a large, but manageable garden for her. It's nice and private, bordered by a stone wall on the road side, the river at the bottom and our fields on the other side."

The road widened as they neared the junction they'd passed when they arrived, and Alan turned the car right, up and over the humpback bridge before turning in at an old gateway on the right and pulling up alongside a low, stone built barn. It was single story, built of large, grey stone blocks, similar to the farmhouse, with slates on the roof and a brick chimney stack at one end.

"That's a new addition," explained Alan, pointing to it. "Most of the conversion was already done, but we improved it all, it hadn't been touched for years." The front had two windows, either side of a large oak panel where once there would have been huge doors through which cattle entered. In the centre of the panel, there was an oak door that opened to reveal Nain, smiling broadly at the gathering, as Dash nipped out from behind her and ran round the children excitedly.

"Welcome, welcome! Come along in," called Nain, beckoning to everyone. "I've been baking, so I hope you have room for something to eat." The four children grinned and all headed inside. Alan went to get the lawn mower so he could cut the grass in Nain's garden.

"It's so cosy!" said Jenny as she looked round the kitchen. "It's like the farmhouse, but on a smaller scale."

"Well, yes, that is what I wanted," replied Nain, pleased that Jenny was so approving of her home. "I'd lived at Pen Y Bryn for all of my life, so I wanted to bring a sense of it here."

"It's hard to imagine that it was once just a barn in a field," added James, "It's a proper little house now."

"It's had a few uses, has this barn," replied Nain. "We converted it from a barn into a youth hostel type place, oh, a good few years ago now, must be at least 30. A local activity centre used to use it as a base for their outdoor activities. They closed down, maybe 10 years ago, and it'd stood empty since. It's nice to have new life in the old place. I remember my grandfather putting the cattle in here in the harsh winters we used to have. Help him, I did, they were very different times back then, everything done by hand. But now, come and look at the garden, we'll sit out and eat gingerbread or brownies, how does that sound?" The four all agreed, enthusiastically and Nain led them through the barn to the glazed, double back doors that looked out onto a stone patio area and expanse of lawn which fell away towards the river. Alan was busy cutting the grass, and the four spilled out of the barn, making straight for the river at the bottom.

"Be careful!" called Alan. "I don't want to be fishing soggy children out!"

"We will!" shouted back Barrie, as the four descended down some stone steps set into the lawn, and arrived at a wooden stage. It was a large flat area, with a narrower deck, leading down from it to just above the water's edge.

"Oh, it's lovely!" exclaimed Liz. "It's like a proper decked area, like a little pier or jetty. You could sit here and dangle your feet over the edge into the water," she added as she stepped down onto the lower level.

There was a small wooden table and two chairs on the main stage which Nain came and joined the children at.

"There are a set of floor cushions in the shed, Bar, would you mind?" Barrie ran off with Jenny to get the cushions and soon they were all sat round on the deck, with Barrie's dad joining his nain on a chair.

"A lot of this stage was unsafe," explained Alan. "We replaced all the rotten timbers and re planked it. It's made quite a nice seating area, don't you think?"

"It's wonderful," said Liz, who was always happiest outside round nature. "You could sit here for hours and just watch what swims or flies past." pointing to a large dragonfly hovering on the opposite bank. "The sound of the water is so soothing too. Even the bridge looks so pretty with wall flowers growing from it."

"I do that," replied Nain. "If you are lucky, you may see a kingfisher. I have spotted one on a few occasions now, between the bend and the bridge." The four all gazed intently, eager to spot a flash of blue and orange that would announce the presence of the elusive bird.

"That's quite a sharp bend in the river" mused James looking upstream. "It's amazing that we're not more than a mile or so from Tully Hall, and there's no evidence of it at all, we can't see one bit of it. Yet, when we were up at the top of the mountain yesterday, you could see the farmhouse, the hall and this barn all quite clearly."

"Yes, you don't have to go far to lose sight of things close to you round here," replied Nain. "It winds a lot, does this river, as the rocks round here are so hard, the river had to run where the rocks denoted rather than carve a path through them, which it would if beneath the ground was something soft, like sandstone. Apparently it makes it more fun for doing activities in."

"Oh, like the ones the hostel people did? Tell us more about the activity centre please Nain," said Barrie, who'd not heard of it before.

"Well, I don't know that much about it really," said Nain, thinking back. "Your Taid used to deal with it mainly. I met two of the leaders, a lovely young man from the next valley over, and a girl, I don't know where she was from, but pleasant enough. We only saw them at the beginning and end of the season, when they came to Pen Y Bryn for things stored in the big barn. Small groups of children, about your age, would stay for a week and would sleep in a dormitory in this barn. They would do a different activity each day, but were generally outdoors, whatever the weather. Worn out at the end of every day, they were, and I imagine by the end of the week, they could have slept for another week!"

"What sort of things did they do?" asked James, "We could perhaps do a few of them ourselves."

"They did a lot of walking, I know that," said Nain. "Gorge walking was up at the head of the valley, and they used to make a little dam in the stream near Pen Y Bryn to look at what creatures were in the water. Even up there they could find tiny fish and the odd crayfish. Round the head of the valley, there are some good rock faces that were rigged for climbing and abseiling down, I know that was always a popular day. Let me think now, oh yes, there was orienteering or map reading which was set up a bit like a treasure hunt over the mountainside and down into the next valley, so they had to work as part of a team." Nain paused, closing her eyes as she thought back, "Oh yes, there was canoeing or kayaking, if you look at the bottom of the little jetty, here you can see mooring rings. They brought the canoes here and then canoed up and down river."

"Oh I wish they were still here!" Barrie said, and the others agreed. "It sounds very like the outward bounds trip we get to go on next term at school. I can't wait for that."

"We could still do some of the things," suggested James, "Gorge walking, and orienteering are doable."

Alan looked doubtful, "I'm not sure," he said. "It's one thing doing it as part of an organised event, quite another for you just to go off alone." His voice trailed off as the excited children all clamoured that they would be safe.

Nain, who was of a mind that children should be able to take care of themselves and no harm can come from exploring the local area, proved to be an ally, "There were several copies of their orienteering maps left when they shut down," she said. "I'd put them away in a drawer in case they ever came in useful. The children can't come to much harm with a map, Al, besides, they all seem to have mobile phones nowadays, they could ring if there was a problem," she said, adding hastily,

"Which there won't be." Alan rolled his eyes and grinned ruefully, an expression that Barrie knew would mean they would be allowed to go off.

"Come on Bar, it's time for tea and some cake," said his nain. "We can eat out here, it's such a lovely day again. Can you help me get the things? We'll get the maps out too." Barrie jumped up and Liz joined him. The three of them headed up to the barn, and soon were back, laden with trays piled high with delicious buns, gingerbread, brownies and biscuits. Barrie had a folder under his arm containing the maps, and, as the children ate, washing the cakes down with tea and juice, they examined them with interest. Nain pointed out the various mountains that rose up steeply beyond her barn, showing them on the map where each one was.

"I'll pack you up plenty of these biscuits and cakes to take with you, keep your energy levels up for all this mountaineering," said Nain, kindly.

"This will be great fun to do," said James, "it's a shame the canoes are not still here."

Nain let out such an exclamation that all the children and Alan stared at her in surprise.

"What is it Nain?" asked Barrie, looking with concern at his gran, her brow furrowed as she concentrated hard.

"I've just remembered," Nain replied, her hand on her forehead, as if to help draw the memory out. "Let me think now, I'm sure. Yes, I think so." The four waited impatiently for her to continue, "The two instructors kept their own canoes in our barn at Pen Y Bryn, theirs were a bit more fancy than the other ones. At the start of their season they would paddle them down from the barn to here, and paddle them back at the end. I don't know why, but I have a feeling that when the company folded, they took the ones the children used from here, but were not interested in taking those from our barn. Yes, I'm sure now, I remember your taid saying about them, Bar."

The four children all talked over each other in their excitement.

"Are they still there?"

"What happened to them?"

"Where are they now?"

Nain laughed at their excited faces.

"I don't know for certain where they are, the last I know of, they were in the big barn, but that must be 10 years ago now, anything could have happened."

"I've not been in that barn," added Alan. "There's a large padlock on the door, for which I've not got the key, and I haven't had the time or need to go into there yet."

"May we please look, Dad?" asked Barrie "We could clear out the barn for you at the same time."

"If we can get the lock off, I don't see why not," replied Alan.

"The lock," considered Nain. "All the keys were usually hung up in the workshop I think, so try there first. I don't know if the canoes are in there, mind. Don't go getting all excited, it might be empty for all I know."

The children were not to be discouraged however, and as they set off for a walk with Nain around the hillside near her home, only one thing was on their minds; getting back to Pen Y Bryn after lunch and getting into that barn.

Chapter Seven

Barn Find

All thoughts of orienteering had gone from the children's minds that afternoon; finding the key was their first task and they met it with enthusiasm. The barn doors were indeed padlocked shut and, circling the barn, the children could find no way in. There were a number of small holes in the walls of the barn for ventilation, but all those they could reach were blocked up on the inside, so they couldn't even get a glimpse of the mysterious interior. The small stone-built workshop situated on the same side of the yard as the farmhouse easily accommodated the four but, as James said, looked like it hadn't been cleared out for years and years. Tools of all descriptions were piled everywhere, on benches, under benches; there were chests of drawers and shelves, boxes, bags and cupboards.

"Nain said the keys were hanging up, or so she thought," said Barrie, scanning the walls

"There's a bunch hanging up here!" called Jenny.

"Here's a ring with two on," added Liz.

"We need to do this methodically," suggested James. "Let's divide the space into four, and each concentrate on our own quarter, collect every key you can find, then hopefully we will have the key we need."

"That's a good idea," agreed Barrie and quickly assigned areas. The four set to work and an hour passed quickly as they looked into every box, drawer and cupboard. Sarah came with drinks for them, and soon there was a growing pile of keys in the middle of the workbench.

It took the children two hours to search the shed thoroughly from top to bottom, they stood, dirty and smiling, looking at their pile of keys. Barrie counted them,

"Forty-seven keys!" he exclaimed, "What on earth did Taid want with that many?"

"Let's go and look at the lock," suggested James, "We will be able to discount a good many of the keys if we know what size of lock it is to fit."

They crossed the farmyard to the barn. The massive doors in the centre were indeed held fast with a padlock. It was old, and of black iron. Barrie slid the protective metal cover to the side, exposing the keyhole.

"It has a pin in the centre of the hole," he said, and the others crowded to look. "So we need a key that has a hole in the end and is about this big," using his thumb and forefinger to show the gap in the padlock.

They brought the keys from the workshop into the sunny farmyard and sat on the cobbles to spread them out. Pretty soon, they had seven keys which they considered to be potential matches for the padlock.

"Moment of truth," said Barrie, as they crossed back to the barn.

"This is so exciting," whispered Liz. "There could be anything in here, just think, we are about to go where no one has gone for years!"

"Why are you whispering?" asked Barrie, as he slid the first key into the lock.

"I don't know, I feel all nervous," whispered back Liz. "It feels right to whisper."

"This one won't go all the way home," said Barrie, handing it to Jenny as James passed him the second key to try. "Need one with a deeper hole in the end."

The second, third and fourth key all failed to fit the lock but, on offering up the fifth, Barrie gave a sharp intake of breath. "It fits!" he cried, only to utter, frustrated a moment later, "but it won't turn!"

"Let me try," offered James. "It's probably just stiff after all these years." James gently tried to turn the key, "Yes, it's seized solid," he announced. "It needs oil spraying in to lubricate it."

"Dad!" shouted Barrie, almost deafening the others, as he spotted his father crossing the yard from the byre. "Dad! Have you got any oil?" Alan came over and tried the lock himself,

"Yes, it is seized," he agreed, "I'll go and get some oil." He soon returned with a can that had a long nozzle, and inserted it into the keyhole. Pressing a little lever on the can he filled the keyhole with oil, until the children saw it pouring out of the hole. "Leave it for a bit to work. If you rush it, you'll snap the key, then you really will be up the creek without a paddle let alone a canoe," he said, laughing at his own joke. "Come into the orchard and pick some fruit for us," he added, knowing the children would be unable to resist trying the lock if they were left by it. "I'll let you know when it's time to try the lock, don't worry. I'm quite keen myself to see what's in the barn now."

The four went into the orchard, where a dozen stunted apple and plum trees grew in rough rows, and spent half an hour picking some of the early ripe apples and plums.

"These are lovely and juicy," said Jenny, as juice dribbled down her chin, "I do love plums, they're always so sweet, apples can be so hit and miss." They soon had a basket full of fruit which Sarah accepted gratefully, saying that it would be plum crumble for pudding that night. The children thought she was superb and told her as much.

"Come on then, you lot! Let's try this lock!" called Alan, beckoning to the four. Excited, they ran over and watched as Alan offered the key to the padlock and began to gingerly turn it. "It's trying, I can feel it starting to give a bit," he said, the others held their breath.

Suddenly there was a grating sound, followed by a loud click. All eyes were focussed on the padlock. Was that the lock opening, or something snapping inside it? The four exchanged nervous glances.

"Ta da!" announced Alan, as the shank of the lock released, and he was able to slide it free from the hasp on the barn door. "Now, I'll just put a drop of oil on the hinges and we'll go in!" The four waited, impatiently, as Alan offered the can up to each of the four huge hinges in turn squirting oil over each moving part. "There," he declared, "open sesame! Come on everyone, we'll all pull together." What would the barn contain? Would there be two fine canoes just waiting to be put back onto the river? What exciting finds awaited them, the children could hardly contain themselves.

Ten hands took hold of the hasp and door itself, slowly easing it open. It creaked loudly, in spite of the oil, for it was old and immensely heavy. "It's coming," panted Alan, as the door slowly swung open, allowing sunlight to flood the barn for the first time in years and years. "In you go," said Alan, standing back. "It's your adventure really. I'll come and have a look later. Shout me if you need anything, I'll be in the byre."

The four stepped inside the huge old building. Ahead of them in the wall opposite was another huge set of doors.

"I bet one of the last two keys fits the lock on that door," said James, "so the barn can be entered from either the fields or the farmyard. We could open that side too and let even more light and air in."

"Yes, but never mind that now," said Barrie, who was eager to explore. Stacked high to the right of the four, were hundreds of bales of hay taking up most of that half of the barn. Cobwebs hung down from them, and a few mice scuttled from view as the children approached. Turning to their left, there was no sign of any canoes, but it was difficult to see in the dim light. Barrie could make out the shape of an old tractor. Not the type seen on modern farms nowadays, this one was small and red, covered in a thick layer of dust, and didn't have a cab, just a seat, open to the elements.

"This would be great to get going!" he shouted excitedly. "I wonder if one of those other keys fits it."

"It doesn't look new enough to need a key," replied James, "but speaking of keys, I'll just go and oil the other lock, then we can get those doors open too perhaps and make it easier to see." Jenny and James went to try and open the other doors, while Barrie and Liz began to slowly clear a passage through past the tractor, to see what else the barn held. Clouds of dust were kicked up, as well as the odd frightened bird that had nested in the barn and was now disturbed by the children's presence, prompting coughs and cries from Barrie and Liz that had the others hurrying with their task to get more fresh air into the barn. The second of the two keys James tried fitted the lock and, after pouring oil into the keyhole, the lock, like the first one, sprang open. James copied Alan's oiling of the hinges and, unleashing the hasp, Jenny and he went back inside the barn.

"Come and help us to push," James called, and Barrie and Liz joined him and Jenny at the inside of the other door. It was not as stiff as the first door and swung open more easily, allowing more light to flood the barn's interior.

"Great! Now we can really see what we're doing," said Barrie and the four went back to exploring the items with interest. There were bits of machinery, wheels, cogs, some ladders with the odd rung missing and an old large flat wooden cart, complete with wooden wheels, which had once been pulled by horses. The harness for this, Liz spotted hanging on huge pegs on the wall. "I've seen an old photo of Taid on a cart behind two great shire horses," said Barrie, "I bet this was the cart, it would be great to get a big horse to pull it now. Gosh this place is really interesting." The others agreed, though, search as they did, there was no sign of the canoes, not even any paddles, and they couldn't help feeling just a bit disappointed after all their hard work and excitement. They sat down on some hay bales that were near the doorway.

"Well, it was worth a try," said Liz, who always liked to be positive. "And it's been fun exploring in here, and we've Tully Hall to explore, and the mountains, we didn't need the canoes."

"Yeah, you're right," said Barrie, "Nain wasn't sure, she'd said that. Plus we have heaps to do."

"I think," began Jenny, then stopped as a hissing noise could clearly be heard. "What's that?" The noise came again and they all listened intently, trying to pinpoint the source.

"It's coming from up high," said James, and they all looked up towards the top of the haystack. There, right at the top, a pair of green eyes from within an orange and black face looked down on them with suspicion, and, as they watched in amazement, the mouth below opened, and the hiss was heard again.

"A cat!" said Jenny in surprise, "I didn't know you had a cat, Bar!"

"I didn't know either!" replied Barrie. "There always used to be one or two about when I used to visit, but they were wild. Nain used to put food out for them, I guess here is where one lives. There will be plenty of mice for it in here, and the ventilation holes we couldn't reach would be easy access for it."

Liz jumped up and went over to the ladder, leaning against the old cart.

"Give me a hand with this, I want to climb up and see the cat," she said,

"I wouldn't if I were you," warned Barrie, "if it's as wild as it looks, it might go for you." Animal mad Liz, however, was not to be dissuaded. Imagining the trouble he would be in with his father if Liz were to get hurt, Barrie helped her get the ladder and position it safely against the stack at the opposite side to where the cat, now disappeared, had been seen. He offered, gallantly, to go up first, but Liz politely declined. "I'll only be a minute," she said. "Hold the ladder, please someone." James and Barrie both took hold of the ladder. "Mind the missing rungs," reminded James. "There's the wire still to stand on, but they'll feel different to the wood, keep it in mind when you are coming down, so you don't fall." "I hope I don't regret this," muttered Barrie, adding, more loudly, "be careful!"

Liz tested the strength of the first rung before putting her weight on it.

"I'll be fine," she said reassuringly, before ascending up, towards the wildcat, making soothing noises as she went, and calling to it. Gingerly, Liz swung from the ladder onto the top of the stack.

"I can't see it," she called down, "I'll go to where it was!" and with that, Jenny disappeared out of sight.

A great whoop and cry of surprise from somewhere on the haystack startled the others greatly.

"What is it?!" shouted up Barrie. "What's wrong, are you hurt?"

"You'll never guess!" called back Liz, still nowhere to be seen. "Come on up."

"You go, Bar," said James, graciously, "it's your barn." So up Barrie went, while James and Jenny held the ladder steadily, wondering what Barrie would find when he got up there.

"I bet it's kittens," suggested Jenny, James remained silent, looking up as Barrie disappeared from view.

Another great cry from somewhere in the haystack was heard.

"What is it?" called up Jenny, "Are there kittens?"

"No kittens, sorry," said Liz, her head appearing over the stack. "James, If I come down, can you join Bar up there, you're stronger than me."

James, completely mystified, held the ladder as Liz descended and quickly climbed it himself as the girls held it still.

"What is it?" demanded Jenny, "I'm the only one that doesn't know now!"

"You'll see in a second," said Liz. "It's more exciting than any kittens, I can tell you."

The sound of bales being moved could be heard and the boys panted with the effort. The front of the stack was higher than the rear by several bales, and as the girls watched, a gap began to appear and enlarge below where the cat had been seen. There was the noise of something being slid over the bales, and, to Jenny's great surprise, from the new gap emerged the front end of a bright blue canoe!

"A canoe!" she shouted. "Are they both there? Gosh, what were they doing up there? How lucky you went up after the cat, Liz! How can we get them down?"

"They're both here," answered Barrie, "There were stacked to the side, I guess so they wouldn't be damaged, but were not in the way, then the hay was stacked round them. They each take two people, I thought they would be single ones, but they aren't. There are four sets of paddles here too and a large canvas bag of something. I think we'll need Dad's help to get them down, Jen, can you run and get him please?"

While Jenny fetched Barrie's father, the boys explored the canvas bag. Inside it were two helmets and two buoyancy aid jackets, with zips up the front.

"These must have been the instructors' own," said Barrie, "They might fit us, be a bit big for the girls perhaps. We'll get it all down and look."

Alan came into the barn and listened to the excited group as they told the tale of finding the canoes.

"Ok," he said, after their request for help retrieving the canoes, "Bar, James, if you get hold of the rear of them, and slowly slide them off the stack, I'll catch the front as they come down and will lower them safely."

The two did as instructed and, in not very many minutes at all, two very smart canoes, one blue, one green, four paddles and the canvas bag lay on the cobbled farmyard in the late afternoon sun.

There was just one hurdle left to jump, getting Barrie's father to allow them to play with them on the river.

Chapter Eight

Exciting Ideas

Examining the canoes was interrupted by Sarah, calling from the farmhouse, "Dinner is ready in ten minutes guys! Come in and wash, I've not seen dirtier children in my life! Al, do you want to go and get Nain? I spoke to her earlier on the phone, she enjoyed this morning so much, I thought it would be nice for her to have dinner with us all."

"Oh fantastic!" cried Barrie, and the others added their approval. Barrie's nain was certainly a welcome addition to any meal or event and, as Barrie thought to himself, might prove to be a useful ally in what he was hoping to propose over dinner.

Soon, with hands and faces washed, the children were all sat round the large kitchen table with Barrie's father and Nain, as Sarah served up another one of her delicious meals; Toad in the hole, with steamed vegetables and roast potatoes. It smelled wonderful and all the children suddenly realised how hungry they were.

"Help yourself to gravy please," she said, sitting down herself, "I've barely seen you today, Katie is quite dependant at the moment, so I'm with her most of the time. Tell me what you have been up to; have you had a good day? I see the barn doors are open."

The four all took it in turns to tell her about their day; the enjoyable morning spent with Barrie's nain, who beamed as they enthused about her baking, the hunting for keys, the opening of the barn and finally the exciting discovery of the two canoes.

"I must put some food out for the cat," said Sarah, "I'd love to see it about the place if we can get it to be less timid."

The conversation lulled and Barrie, looking at his father to gauge his reaction, pondered out loud how great it would be to be able to paddle the canoes on the little river in the lovely hot summer weather. He saw his father stiffen in his seat, and his jaw muscles clench slightly. This wasn't going to be as easy as Barrie had hoped.

"You can put that thought right out of your head, Barrie Williams," said Alan firmly. "It's far too dangerous. Anything could happen, and I will not be held responsible for you all drowning in the name of having a bit of fun messing about on the river. There's lots to do here to occupy your time, you've Tylluan Hall to explore on Wednesday and I'm going to town in the morning if you'd all like a look around there."

Barrie looked a bit crestfallen. He had expected some resistance, but an outright refusal had come as a bit of a shock.

"We'd be very careful," he began as the other children sat in silence, not wanting to interfere with this family disagreement. "Honestly, Dad."

"Out of the question," replied his father, getting up to quieten Katie, who had begun to cry in her crib. Picking her up and soothing her, before gently replacing her, he returned to the table, "Finish your meal."

The children ate in silence. The atmosphere was uncomfortable and Barrie's nain, unable to stand it, cleared her throat and spoke.

"Well, I think you're being completely hypocritical, Alan. Was it not you who built the raft and paddled up the river to visit

Bar's mam here when you were only his age? I seem to remember the two of you spending many an afternoon with it moored here sat picnicking on it, and sitting with your bare feet in the water. In fact," she added, warming to her cause "did I not look you out a pair of my husband's old trousers and an old shirt after you fell in and came up to the farm looking like a drowned rat?"

Alan visibly reddened. "It, it was different back then," he muttered, struggling to think of what to say in reply.

"How? Was the water not as wet?" asked Nain, adding a smile to soften her challenge. "You were then as these four are now, young and full of adventure. Let them paddle, what harm can it do?"

"Drowning!" retorted Alan.

"They can have life jackets or whatever they wear to do that sort of thing," persisted Nain, "Far more than you wore when you were rafting, and you were ok."

"What do you think, Sarah?" asked Alan, in a vain hope to get some support from his wife. To his disappointment, Sarah sided with Nain, seeing how keen the children were, and how much joy just finding the canoes had brought to Barrie, who she was so very fond of.

"Well, I can see where your loyalties lie!" he replied, with a loud harrumph, breaking into a smile. Putting his hands up in the air in a gesture of surrender, he added "Okay, okay, I'm outnumbered. But, and this is a big but. Firstly, we need to have permission from all of your parents for you to do this, and secondly, we need to source you all the appropriate safety gear. I'm not allowing any of you in the water without helmets and buoyancy jackets. I'm not being a killjoy, or a mood hoover, I just care, that's all."

"Mood hoover!" repeated Jenny, and went into such a fit of laughter that soon, everyone round the table had tears running down their cheeks from laughing so hard. Barrie got up and, putting his arm out like a vacuum nozzle, ran round the table tickling people in the ribs with his nozzle arm while making a hoovering noise. Dash capered about him, tripping him up. The mood had changed completely to one of high spirits and silliness, and it took several minutes for everyone to compose themselves enough for pudding.

After everything was cleared away and the dishwasher loaded, Jenny and James went upstairs and got their mobile phones to speak to their parents about canoeing. Liz hadn't yet got her new phone set up, and had been using Jenny's to keep in touch with her mum as her old phone was so temperamental it wasn't worth even attempting a call. Bringing them back down into the kitchen, as the lounge was full of boxes still from the move, James rang his parents. His father answered and they had a brief conversation about how the trip was going and what they had been up to. James had sent some photos of the scenery, taken the previous day from Wolf's Rock, using his phone, and the others could hear his father agreeing how stunning the area was; he shared his son's love for the outdoors. James brought the canoes into the conversation and was pleasantly surprised that his father was in favour of them playing on the river.

Giving his friends the thumbs up, James handed his phone to Alan, who spoke down the phone about the requirement for helmets and life jackets, which they could hear James' father agreeing to. Ending the call and passing the phone back to James, Alan raised his eyebrows, "Well, you heard that, James' father is in agreement regarding the safety precautions, but is of a mind that you can use the canoes. I am outvoted so far."

The children all gave small, nervous laughs as the same idea at once ran through their minds, Barrie voiced it. "Crumbs, what if one of your parents Jenny, Liz, refuses permission? What do we do then?"

The girls looked worried, "Well, you'd have to paddle without either or both of us," said Jenny, graciously, and Liz agreed. "Yes, we would have to run alongside."

"No," said James, looking quite stern for his twelve years. "Do you remember when it looked like you wouldn't be able to come Jenny, and we'd not heard from you, Liz, the first day we planned to come here these hols? Bar and I knew then we couldn't go without either of you. We will always stick as one. Either we all canoe, or none canoe."

"I agree," added Barrie, nodding his head vigorously.

Alan looked at both boys, and couldn't help but be immensely impressed at their mature attitude. He reached over and put a hand on a shoulder of each of them.

"I'm proud, proud of you both." he said, as the girls looked on, hoping their parents would agree.

It was a tense time as Jenny rang her parents and, speaking to them both, went through the same routine James had, handing the phone to Alan.

"Three down, one to go," announced Alan, after a brief conversation, handing Jenny her phone back. "Liz, would you like to use our house phone? I know you're having trouble with yours."

"That's great, thank you. I will get my new phone set up soon," answered Liz, accepting the phone Alan held out to her. She dialled her number and they all heard Mrs Green answer the phone; the other three held their breath.

The conversation could clearly be heard as Liz, telling her mother all about the canoes, mentioned their idea about using them to paddle on the river. The line went quiet. Barrie, crossing his fingers looked concerned. Holding the phone closer to her ear, Liz tried her best to convince her mother. "Yes. No. Of course it's safe. Yes, people have done it for years. We'd have proper equipment, helmets and buoyancy jackets. It's only like what we are to go on next term with school. Uhuh," she fell silent as she listened to her mother's response before starting again, "But everyone else's parents have said yes. Can't you just tell Dad after? Okay. No, I understand. You've got this number? Yes, I'll wait. Love you, bye."

Putting the phone down, she turned to the others.

"Mum said she can't agree without speaking to Dad. He's visiting a friend in hospital, so she can't get him on his mobile, but when he's home, she'll ask him and then call here."

"Did she sound in favour though?" asked James, who was really looking forward to paddling on the river.

"Difficult to say, you heard me saying about the trip we go on next term, and Mum went on it with the year above us last year. Mind you, perhaps I shouldn't have reminded her, Matthew Waddington was messing about, rocking his canoe from side to side, managed to flip it over and bashed his nose on a rock. Mum had rung home that night saying that there was blood everywhere, don't you remember? He came back sporting two black eyes and was called *Panda* for weeks."

The four all sat, staring at the phone. Sarah went upstairs to put Katie to bed in her cot, and Alan left to take Nain and Dash back home. Time ticked slowly on, the old grandfather clock in the hall had been wound up that day, and the pendulum sounded unnaturally loud in the silent house. All four began to yawn, for they had had an exciting day.

Returning downstairs Sarah suggested they get ready for bed, so they could go to sleep as soon as Liz's father had phoned, reassuring them that she would stay by the phone while they did so.

While they were getting washed and changed for bed Alan returned, and soon they were all sat back in the kitchen, willing the phone to ring. Sarah made them all cups of hot chocolate, as the room had cooled and they were only wearing pyjamas. They had nearly finished these, sitting in gloomy silence, when the phone rang, making them jump so much that Liz, sat nearest it, almost fell off her chair.

Seeing on the display that it was her parents' calling, Liz picked up the receiver and, crossing her fingers to the others, answered. Three hands rose up in reply, showing crossed fingers back at her, and, not wanting the children to be disappointed, especially after their impressive attitude around being a team, Alan too solemnly raised a hand with crossed fingers.

Liz didn't say much and, after a few words held the phone out to Alan.

"Dad wants to discuss it with you," she said.

Taking the phone, Alan spoke brightly into it, asking how Liz's Dad's friend was in hospital, and saying what a fine time the children were having and how Liz was a delight to have around. He got up from his chair and walked a little away from the children, who strained their ears to hear what he said. They could make out him telling Liz's dad that the other parents had agreed, and heard helmets and buoyancy jackets mentioned several times. The grandfather clock then chimed loudly to mark nine o'clock, drowning out the end of the conversation, as the children saw Alan press a button on the phone to end the call. He looked very grim.

"I'm sorry kids, I tried my best for you really I did."

"Thank you for trying, we'll just do other stuff, as long as we're together, we'll have fun," said James, bitterly disappointed, but determined not to show it, so that Liz didn't feel guilty. It wasn't her fault her parents had refused permission.

"Yes, I am sure you will," replied Alan, looking at James and three downcast faces, "but that other stuff will have to include a trip to town with me tomorrow to sort out finding where we can hire helmets and buoyancy aids for you all."

"But," began Liz, and the others looked confused.

Alan broke into a wide smile, laughing at the four questioning faces. "I'm sorry, I couldn't resist. I talked him round, and said how sensible you had been and how grown up you all were. He's happy for you to have a paddle as long as you are careful."

All four gave loud cries and yells of excitement, prompting Alan to wave his hands to quieten them.

"Shhh, Katie's asleep. Now, off to bed with you all, or you'll be too tired for paddling tomorrow, assuming of course, we can find a place to get you some kit."

They all hugged him and headed upstairs to their beds knowing one thing. No matter how little sleep they got tonight, they wouldn't be too tired for paddling tomorrow!

Chapter Nine

A Trip to Town

Tuesday morning dawned bright and sunny. The four awoke after a long sleep, refreshed from the day before and all were thinking of one thing; paddling on the river.

The girls got dressed and went downstairs into the large kitchen. Barrie and James were already sat at the table, waiting for them. Barrie had a laptop open and James was looking intently at his tablet.

"You're up and ready early," said Liz, running her hand through her hair, as she had yet to brush it. "We saw you weren't in your room, so came straight down. What are you doing?" Barrie looked up. "Looking for where we might get the jackets and helmets we need for canoeing," he said.

"Nothing in the nearest town," added James, "but here, what do you think of this Bar, Outdoor Adventures? Is that close? It says they hire out canoes, so they must also hire all the bits to go with them."

Barrie looked at the screen James was holding up, "It's about three quarters of an hour away, I think," he said. "Nothing is really close to here, I'll ask Dad what he thinks."

Sarah came in carrying Katie at that point, and Jenny went over to the baby, who was looking around her, smiling.

Setting her down in her crib, Sarah greeted them all, and put the kettle on for morning cups of tea.

"I just can't start the day without one," she said, and Jenny, one of her fingers firmly in Katie's tiny grasp, agreed.

Soon they were all tucking into bowls of cereal and slices of toast. Alan came in and joined everyone at the table. He had been out early clearing the byre, and he explained to the children that getting permission to turn it into cottages would take a while, and so clearing it took priority over some of the work in the farmhouse. James immediately offered to help, and Alan, thanking him, said they could help, but he was heading into town in about an hour. If they wanted to all go with him and see about getting the safety gear for the canoes, they would be welcome.

As soon as breakfast was finished, Barrie showed his father the website James had found. His father agreed that it looked like it was the closest that would be able to meet their needs and said he would take them there that morning.

Clearing away the breakfast things, the four worked quickly to help Sarah with a few chores in the house, before hearing the car horn and heading out into the farmyard. They all got in the large car and headed down the mountain road, passing Tylluan Hall and turning right, past Nain's cottage in a short cut, according to Alan, which took them up and over the mountain. They stopped briefly at the top at the request of Jenny, to take some photographs of the stunning views of the neighbouring valley they now looked down into. The car continued slowly on, as sheep and half grown lambs wandered between fields and along the road, seemingly free to go where they liked. Alan reassured a worried Liz that they didn't stray far and wouldn't come to harm.

"This road is only used by locals, and we all drive slowly – there are signs up warning people, just like there are in the Yorkshire Dales near you."

Opening a little storage compartment in the rear of the car, Jenny gave a happy cry as she found where their sweets from

Saturday had been put, and they all settled down, enjoying a few as the countryside passed them by.

It took nearly an hour to reach the town, and they first had to get some shopping with Barrie's father that Sarah had written on a list.

"Cat food is on it, see what you've started?" he laughed, selecting some tins from a shelf.

Soon, the shopping complete, they headed off in the car to the outdoor shop, about half a mile from the town centre.

"It looks all in darkness!" exclaimed Barrie in disappointment as the car drew up beside a brightly coloured shop with a sign that read *Outdoor Adventures – Everything you need for fishing and walking to climbing and kayaking*. It was indeed all in darkness, the shop was shut! The children all looked at each other, dismally.

"We're doomed!" said Jenny, in a dramatic tone putting her hand up to her head and continuing in the same, theatrical voice. "Fate is putting everything in our path, the trials, the tribulations!" It certainly didn't look promising, and the four stood with their noses pressed against the shop window, as if they could will someone to come out from the back.

"That just makes it worse! Look at this poster," said Barrie, pointing to a brightly coloured A3 poster advertising organised trips which showed a group of children negotiating a section of river in canoes. The water broke white around the rocks in the photograph and spray was flung up, so that the children's faces were a mix of big smiles with wide eyes, and grimaces on those who were about to get wet. It certainly looked like great fun and James reading the poster noticed something that puzzled him.

"The phone number is the same one as it on the front of the shop, look," he said, pointing up at the sign. "The shop must have something to do with it, and it has the address of the river place. Is it far, Sir?" he asked, turning to Alan and still preferring to avoid referring to Barrie's father by his name where possible.

There was a little map included on the poster and looking, Alan replied, "About ten minutes I think. I'll just try the number." He dialled the number, and they could hear a phone inside the shop ring out loudly. No one appeared.

"Well, there is nothing to be gained here, shall we take a trip to the place and see if anyone can help?"

"Thanks Dad!" said Barrie, aware of the time this was taking when his father was busy.

Everyone got back into the car and Alan programmed the satellite navigation system to take them to the address on the poster. The route took them up a steep mountain track, to the left of which fell a sharp ravine. Catching a glimpse of a rushing river at the base of it, Barrie commented that it looked like the rapids, with his father replying that it was a good job their river wasn't that dramatic or they'd not be paddling on it at all.

On and on it went, up into the mountains. Jenny thought they would be in the clouds if they kept going much further, but at last it ended in a large clearing, surrounded by trees which gave the whole place a shaded, green glow. To the right rose a sheer rock face which enclosed the area and made it feel quite sheltered and protected. There were about a dozen cars parked up and several people, wearing life jackets and helmets, could be seem milling about a wooden building. They all got out and Alan went to see if he could find someone in charge. As he disappeared out of sight behind the wooden building, the four chatted excitedly, they were so close to achieving their goal of paddling down the river.

"To think, twenty-four hours ago, we had no thought of paddling down the river, all our attention was on the mystery of Tully Hall," said Liz.

"Yes," added James, "and now it's all we've been talking about, you know, I hadn't thought about Tully Hall once! We really need to keep that mystery in our minds if we are to stand any chance of solving it. I,"

"Dad's waving at us!" interrupted Barrie. The others looked and saw him beckoning them over to the hut.

"This is Tom," he said, gesturing to a smiling man in his twenties. It was obvious to the four that Tom was used to being in the outdoors, for he was tanned and looked very fit.

"Pleased to meet you," said Tom, and extended his hand to shake each of theirs.

"Tom's being ever so kind. He is in charge here and, not only is he willing to hire us everything you need, but he's also offered to give you a half hour session on the water so that you are safe paddling on the river this afternoon."

There were happy shouts from the children as they all thanked Tom effusively. Laughing at their excited faces, Tom shepherded them into the hut.

"Let's get you kitted out."

It didn't take him long to find them all helmets and buoyancy aids that fitted them.

"We'll join you onto this group that are getting into their canoes now, with Andy," said Tom, pointing, and the children saw a similar-looking man helping a young girl get into a two person canoe very like those currently at Pen Y Bryn, in which a boy, about the same age as them, already sat.

Tom lifted two more two person canoes from a steel rack and carried them over to the water. Holding them steady, he gestured for James and Jenny to get in one and, once they were seated safely, he helped Barrie and Liz into the other. He then stood back up and addressed the group as a whole. "You are all sitting in tandem kayaks. These are lightweight and very stable on the water."

So theirs were not canoes after all, but kayaks. They'd learned something already, not that it really made a difference to them.

Tom and Andy then talked everyone through how to paddle, steer and stop safely. Andy was in a single kayak and demonstrated the actions they all should take with the paddles as Tom described them in turn. Each pair had to work together, he explained, for the craft to run smoothly and efficiently on the water. The group all practiced in the calm area of water they were in, moving off and steering their kayaks round in a large ring, before lining up and stopping as a group, a few pairs knocked into other kayaks, and it was good to see how stable they were on the water. Finally, Tom covered what to do in the event of a kayak capsizing, or 'turning turtle' as he phrased it, emphasising and reassuring the group that, unless they hit a rock at speed, which they shouldn't if paying attention, or intentionally tried to, they shouldn't capsize.

Alan took some photographs of the four as they practiced paddling, and joined Tom to help them out, as the group prepared to paddle down the river. Barrie saw Andy removing a net that had been strung across the river, just downstream of where they were and picking up a blue sack, which he dropped into his kayak.

"It's always wise to stop the odd premature paddler," Tom said, seeing where Barrie was looking.

The four and Alan thanked Tom again for his help and Alan assured Tom he would have the helmets and buoyancy aids returned by Saturday.

They loaded the things into the boot of the car and began the journey back to Pen Y Bryn.

"I feel a lot happier, now that you had a little bit of instruction on what to do and how to be safe," Alan said.

"Thanks for organising it, Dad, Tom seemed a really nice person," said Barrie.

"Wasn't he just. He did say you would find paddling up-stream a lot more challenging than paddling down. I wonder, if you are keen to paddle today, whether it should be a one way trip. If you paddled down to Nain's you could moor there, and I could pick you up. The canoes, or rather kayaks, should fit on the roof of the car okay. Nain, I imagine would be happy to sit and look out for you, and could phone me when you arrived safely. We'll call in and speak to her on the way home, we pass her cottage anyway."

"That's a brilliant idea," said Jenny, and James added;

"If there's any rope there, we could tie lengths to the mooring posts we saw yesterday, and grab onto them as we got there. Are there places to tie them to on the can... kayaks?" he corrected. Jenny looked at the photos she had taken of the kayaks the day before, enlarging the image.

"Yes, look, there are little rings near the front."

"Perfect. There is some rope in the shed, I saw it when I got the floor cushions yesterday," said Barrie.

"Gosh I'm hungry," announced Liz, looking forlornly at her empty sweet packet. "Is anyone else? I'm eating masses more than usual as well!" They all agreed they were ravenous, and Alan said it was the good fresh air and that they were also doing more physical activity than they had been at school.

Turning into Nain's gateway Alan brought the car to a halt and got out, saying he'd go himself as they were running late for lunch. Nain opened the door while waving at the car and, lowering his window, Barrie heard his father tell her of their suggestion. Nain was delighted and at once said that she would gladly receive the intrepid paddlers.

"You can come up for dinner with the kayaks!" shouted Barrie. After all, he said to the others, had it not been for Nain they wouldn't have known about the kayaks or been given permission to paddle them.

"Your nain is lovely anyway," said James, "I wish she was my gran, I don't have any."

Alan returned to the car and, waving madly at Nain as they pulled away, they all headed up to Pen Y Bryn where a lunchtime feast and an afternoon's adventure of paddling down the river awaited them. They could hardly wait!

Chapter Ten

Down on the River

It was nearly two o'clock by the time they had finished lunch.
Sarah had got it all ready for their return, and thick slices of
cold meat, coleslaw, salad and crusty bread had quickly been
gobbled down by the excited children as they told Sarah all
about the morning's escapades.

The four got changed into suitable clothing for life on the
water, thin waterproof coats were put on before they all
zipped themselves into their buoyancy aids.

"These are ever so light," commented Liz as she adjusted
hers.

"Well, they would hardly help you be buoyant and float if
they were as heavy as lead now would they?" replied Jenny,
and they all giggled.

Helmets were put on and checked and they all lined up in the
farmyard by the kayaks as Alan took a photograph. Dividing
up the same as they had that morning at the safety brief, each
pair could easily manage to carry a kayak between them and
they all headed down to the river, by the rickety old bridge.
Sarah came along too, carrying Katie, and soon they were
setting the kayaks down in the water. It was little more than
a large stream there at that point, and Alan held each kayak
steady in turn as the pair got in. James and Jenny's blue kayak
sank with their weight, causing it to ground on the rocky
stream bed, but energetic wriggling backwards and forwards
by the pair got the vessel dislodged and afloat in slightly
deeper water. They all wedged their paddles into the rocks

beneath the water and held their kayaks fast while Alan took some photos of them.

"Have a great time and be careful!" he called to them, half wishing he could go as well, with Sarah adding;

"You all look great, have fun. Look out for the kingfishers!" Releasing their paddles the kayaks started slowly downstream, prompting excited whoops from the four. They were off! Hardly believing their luck, the four steadily paddled, soon disappearing out of sight of the grownups round a bend in the stream, it really was great fun already and lovely to be on their own, being able to choose exactly what to do. They carefully avoided the rocks that stood proud of the water while the stream was so shallow, and, on occasion, all had to do a bit of wiggling to re-float grounded kayaks. After not very long at all, the stream widened considerably and no rocks from the bed poked through the water. Several more streams had been entering the water from the opposite mountainside to the farmhouse, flowing underground only to appear a few meters from the river, as the bank fell away.

"Let's stop here and do some practicing," said Barrie, sat at the front of the green kayak. "The water is wide enough here to do turns and deep enough that we won't get grounded. We have all afternoon and it would be a good idea to get really good at this before the river gets bigger and faster." It was agreed, so they all brought their kayaks to a stop, gently back paddling to counteract the slow current that would carry them down the river. The river was faster flowing than where they had tried that morning and it wasn't as easy to manoeuvre the kayaks accurately. They persisted and gradually improved as they learned to work as pairs. It was hard work, but great fun and by the time an hour had passed all the children were panting with the effort, for the sun was strong and they were warm in all their clothing.

"Let's moor up on the side somewhere, can we?" asked Liz, who was about ready for a rest. "I brought some of the brownies your nain made us Bar, thought they make a fine afternoon snack, I know I'm certainly working up an appetite."

"That's a great idea," replied Barrie turning round in his seat. He called over to James and Jenny who were a little downriver and in reply James pointed to a large tree he was next to growing right on the bank of the river whose branches hung down low, dropping so much they almost touched the water in places.

"This will be a perfect spot," called James, "We've nothing to tie the kayaks up with, but we could climb out here and pull them onto the bank, the tree provides a great natural staircase." Barrie and Liz paddled down to him, and could see that the tree, a fine large willow, did indeed make an ideal natural landing, for the exposed roots formed wooden steps up to the bank. Getting out of the kayaks was not as easy without someone to hold them steady, so James, being the biggest and strongest, said he would get out first and so be able to help the others. He and Jenny paddled their kayak under the drooping branches into deep shade and as close as they could get to the trunk of the large willow tree as James got himself in a position where he could climb out. Crouching on his seat, he felt very unstable and as Jenny pushed the kayak as close as possible to the tree, made a great leap for the tangle of roots. The kayak rocked violently and Jenny screamed in terror, fearing it flipping over and soaking her in the cold river. Turning and grabbing the front of the kayak, James fought hard to steady it and gradually the rocking subsided; panic gave way to relieved laughter.

"Heavens to Betsy! I thought you were going in there Jen!" called Liz from the back of her kayak.

"So did I!" called back Jenny as she took James' hand and got safely to the base of the tree. Together they struggled and slowly managed to pull the kayak up the bank and onto the grassy top above, leaving room for Liz and Barrie to bring their kayak to the water's edge. James returned and called to Liz.

"You'd better pass the brownies over to us before you get out!"

"Why on earth should I do that? They're deep in my pockets!" shouted back Liz

"Well, I doubt they'd taste good with river water as a sauce," James said back, laughing as Lizzy glared indignantly.

"I suggest then, that you hold us steady and make sure I stay dry!" she retorted, sticking her tongue out at the laughing James as she and Barrie edged their kayak carefully closer. James held it steady as Barrie climbed out, then turned and offered out his hand for Liz to hold. She took it and safely made it to the old roots of the willow, climbing them up into the sunshine as James and Barrie together brought the second kayak to safety at the top of the bank.

The three threw themselves down beside Jenny, who was laid out on the bank, her eyes shut against the bright afternoon sun.

"This is brilliant isn't it?" asked James, loving being in the outdoors and on their own.

"Definitely," said Barrie, and the girls agreed.

"They're a bit squashed I'm afraid" added Liz, inspecting a paper bag from her pocket and tearing it to reveal four large brownies.

"Oh that doesn't matter a bit," said James.

They sat in silence in the warm July sun, enjoying the rich chocolate brownies.

"It's just missing a nice cool drink, I should have thought to bring some, there's space around our feet," said Liz

"We can bring drinks next time," said Barrie. "Today isn't going to be the only day we spend on the water, I'm sure. I should have thought when we were at the centre this morning, did you see the pack on the back of Andy's kayak? It was a sort of waterproof bag which was strapped to the back, we've got the fastenings on ours, look. I should have asked if they had a spare bag."

"A bag by our feet will do fine, I'm sure," said James, "We'll bring a rope next time too and tie it to the round the tree so we can moor the kayaks to it," he added, and the others agreed.

"We will have to keep an eye out for Tylluan Hall," said Barrie. "We mustn't forget that, and you never know, we might spot something, looking at it from a different angle. I don't know what we'll be able to see from the water."

"Well, let's go and find out," said Liz, standing up and stretching.

Refreshed by their snack and break, they lowered the kayaks down to the water. James and Barrie carried the green one first and James held it still as Liz and Barrie sat down and got settled. Then James and Jenny brought theirs down and James held it as Jenny climbed in. She looked rather nervous and James was a bit worried how he would climb aboard without rocking the kayak again. He managed it, getting a wet left foot, and was soon safely in. They emerged from the deep shade of the willow tree just in time to hear a cry from Liz, "My paddle!"

She'd dropped it in the river and, fortunately being made of plastic it was floating, but floating away from her and Barrie, who was quite helpless with laughter.

"Come on Jen, let's get it! Paddle as fast as you can!"

Jenny and James shot off in their kayak after the paddle and it was quite surprising how fast they managed to go. They could only keep it up for a short distance though, and really had to push hard to catch up with the paddle. James at the front, reaching out with his paddle, managed to snare it and brought Liz's paddle safely aboard. A round of applause could be heard from Liz and Barrie, as Jenny and James turned their kayak round and began to paddle back to them. Barrie's father had been right, paddling against the current was hard work, but doable, as long as they went slow and steady. It would be a challenge to go the whole way back from Nain's though, they were both glad the car would carry them home.

"Your paddle, M'lady," said James, as they pulled alongside Liz, lowering his head in a mock bow.

Liz took the paddle and, lowering it, knighted James, "Arise Sir James, guardian of the lost paddle," she laughed.

"Let's head off to the Hall then, we need to have enough time to see what we can from the river," said Barrie, and, all composed and settled, the four steadily paddled down the river. It was such a lovely way to spend the afternoon, and they pointed out little animals that they saw running along the banks. James spotted several water voles and sharp eyed Liz swore she'd seen an otter.

"I think the grounds of the hall should be just round this next corner," said Barrie as they approached quite a sharp left hand bend in the river, "it can't be very much further."

It wasn't, and rounding the bend the four got their first sight of the grounds of Tylluan Hall, or rather the very edge of them, for a high brick wall formed the bank of the river to their left, extending high enough to stop them being able to look over.

"Rats," said Barrie, "that must be how the grounds are so flat, the land has been levelled and is held in place by the wall. Well, that's foxed us being able to do a bit of spying from the river.

"Never mind," said Liz, behind him. "We'll have it solved by tomorrow, I bet."

They paddled slowly on, looking at the wall with interest. "Look how small the bricks are," observed James, "I bet it's ever so thick if it's holding back the actual grounds from slipping into the river." Anything further he was going to say was cut off by an excited shout from Barrie, who was a little ahead, and rounding a slight left bend.

"Gosh! Look at this! It's a secret passage! James, Jenny, look!" In a few moments James and Jenny joined him and Liz and all four stared at what had caused Barrie such excitement. There, in the brick wall of the river bank, was an archway. Its top was about five feet above the waterline and it was about three feet wide; a passageway in the side of the river.

"What on earth is it for do you think?" asked Barrie, but the others couldn't guess.

After a few moments thinking James suggested, "That large lake we could see from Wolf's rock, could it be the overflow for that do you think?"

"Well, yes, it could be," considered Barrie "But it seems an awful lot of work to go to, just as an overflow, I want to see where it leads."

"Can we paddle up it do you think?" said Jenny feeling the hairs on the back of her neck rise up in excitement.

"We have to try!" said Barrie, nosing his kayak into the mouth of the passage. "The water's certainly deep enough, though it is pitch black, I can't see a thing. Has anyone got a torch on them?"

Nobody did, though James's phone had a built in torch and, he tried to pass it to Liz, who was in the entrance of the passageway. In a terrifying moment the phone slipped from his hand just as he went to put it into Liz's grasp and, bouncing up from her palm they both scrabbled wildly in the air for it knocking it up as they tried desperately to keep it from going into the water. Mercifully, as time seemed to slow down, it bounced back into James' lap and letting his breath out in a long sigh of relief, he carefully replaced it in his pocket.

"My heart was in my mouth then," said Jenny, breaking the tension everyone had felt.

"Yours was? Imagine mine!" said James, who had saved hard and bought his phone himself earlier in the year. "We need to come back, properly prepared Bar, with torches, or a head torch, and explore this place properly, spend some time on it.

Don't forget also, your nain is waiting for us, if we cause them any worry now, we'll not be allowed again."

Reluctantly Barrie, seeing the sense in James' advice, reversed the kayak out of the passageway. It was easy, tucking his paddle in the kayak, he spread his arms out, and pushed backwards along the side walls of the passage.

The two pairs paddled side by side as they continued down, surprised at how quickly the time had passed. Their only topic of conversation was the secret passageway, and how they would explore it, where it would lead to and what it might contain.

"We simply must make it down there," implored Liz, who was desperate to discover what secrets were held within.

"Your nain might know, or Sarah, working at the hall, she's as good a person to ask as anyone. What do you think, shall we ask them over dinner?" put in Jenny

The others considered. "I'm inclined to say no, we don't ask them," said Barrie, frowning. "For the same reason we agreed when up at Wolf's Rock not to ask James' dad about the mystery, do you remember? They'd put a stop to it, I'm sure. Look how hard we had to try to get them to agree about us paddling on the river. If we said we were exploring a secret passageway that had been forgotten for years and was accessible only by the river, they would either want to be involved, or, more likely be boring and grown up like and just stop us coming on the river again. So I really think we ought not to tell them anything about it, let it be our proper secret, what do you think?"

There was silence for a few minutes as the others reflected.

"We can't lie to them," started James, "so we will just avoid the subject, which won't be difficult as they don't know anything about it."

"Yes, I agree, I couldn't lie, but we can talk about the picnic, the paddle, the otter sighting," continued Jenny and Liz agreed.

They started discussing what they would need to bring to explore the passage, and where they could get things. Barrie's dad had a head torch, but Barrie hadn't seen it since the move and there was an old torch in the kitchen, in case the power went off. They badly wanted to return to it in the morning, but as Barrie had reminded them, they were going to Tylluan Hall tomorrow, which would be ideal as they could look for the land side of the passageway then, if indeed it came out in the grounds and was not just an overflow from the huge lake.

"Gosh look!" said James, as they rounded a bend, everyone stared where he pointed and there, perched by the side of the river with the unmistakable blue and orange iridescent plumage, was a magnificent kingfisher. None of the four had seen one in real life before and they looked in wonder at such a stunning bird and watched, open mouthed, as it flew off downriver.

"What a treat!" exclaimed Liz, wishing she'd had her new phone with her and been able to take a photograph of it.

"Hey look, there's the little staging. We've made good time on this last bit," pointed Barrie, and waved wildly from the front of the kayak. Waving back, his nain watched, beaming as they successfully managed to reach the mooring ropes and secure their kayaks. She had tied long lengths of rope to them so it was easy for the children to do.

"My, what a lovely sight that was to see, you all looking so happy as you paddled down. Did you see the kingfisher? It flew past here just ahead of you."

"Yes, I think we startled it, Nain. Sorry if we took longer than you may have thought, we have been practising how to paddle and stopped off at the most amazing place."

"Yes, a large willow tree with roots like a staircase," cut in James, worried that Barrie might be about to give the game away.

Nain listened with pleasure at the tales of adventure and fetched out a large pitcher of ice cold orange juice, which quenched the thirst of the four. They had only just finished their drinks when Alan arrived and helped the tired children carry the kayaks up to the car, securing them to the roof rack. "You must be worn out," he said, looking at four tired, smiling faces.

"They are, cariad bach," said Nain softly, "I'll not come for dinner tonight if it is ok with you Al, I'm quite tired myself, and I think these four would do best with supper, a bath and an early night."

So the four headed up, and enjoyed another beautiful meal, telling Sarah and Alan about the wildlife they had seen and asking for some rope so they could fasten it round the willow tree next time. No one mentioned the secret passageway and, after yawning with tiredness, they excused themselves and went to their bedrooms to discuss the mystery of the passageway in the wall. Whatever happened tomorrow, they were determined to return to the river as soon as ever they could and see where that passageway took them, a real adventure.

Chapter Eleven

Tylluan Hall

It was an early start for the four on Wednesday; at 08:00am Sarah was tapping gently on their doors. They had slept fitfully, discussing in their pairs the strange arch in the brick wall, and where the passageway may lead, long into the night. All were deeply asleep when their alarms had sounded, and remained so until woken half an hour later by Sarah's arrival.

Hurriedly they all washed and dressed, fighting over the bathroom and getting in each other's way before running helter-skelter down the stairs and bursting into the kitchen, hair still on end.

Full of apologies they set themselves down at the table, where cereal and toast awaited them.

"It's ok, I expect you were exhausted from your paddling yesterday," said Sarah, knowing nothing of their late night hushed conversations and excitement of finding the passageway.

"It was great fun, thanks for helping to persuade Dad," said Barrie

"Oh you're welcome, I'm just glad you enjoyed it. I will just go and see to Katie, we need to leave in time to get to the Hall by quarter to nine, so I can have fifteen minutes to give you a whistle stop tour before I start work. You will be free to wander about and explore the place, and I think your Dad said something about Jake offering to show you round parts, so we'll find him before I start work too."

The four ate quickly. Alan had already had his breakfast and was working at his computer in the lounge, his desk nestled among the boxes, ready to look after Katie while Sarah worked at the Hall.

Having all loaded the dishwasher and brushed both teeth and hair, Barrie shouted goodbye to his father and the children went into the farmyard where Sarah was waiting in the car.

It only took a few minutes to reach the Hall and, entering between huge stone pillars the four got their first proper look at the place, as Sarah drove slowly down the drive towards it. Tylluan Hall was built entirely of stone, and, thought Jenny, looked more like a castle than a hall, with castellations all round and a great tower that rose up from the centre. Built of mainly grey stone with lighter beige stone used on the corners and around the windows and doors, it really was very commanding. Huge chimney stacks pointed up towards the bright summer sky, blackened around their tops from years of smoky fires burning beneath them.

Sarah brought the car to a halt just to the right of the front door, and the four got out, completely awed by the building in front of them.

The majority of the building was two storeys high, with the tower adding a third. The main entrance to the Hall had a most impressive large gothic arched oak double door, decorated all over with black ironwork and studs. The windows were of leaded glass which gave them quite a dark appearance too. The whole place had a gothic, brooding air to it and Jenny shivered, in spite of the warm July sun.

"It is quite intimidating," she said, and the others agreed.

"Looks almost medieval," added Liz, her knowledge of history coming from her mum's love of the subject.

"It had quite a few different influences when it was built, you're right," replied Sarah, lifting her bags from the car and heading towards the entrance, her feet crunching on the stone chipping drive. "Come on in, you'll soon see it is nothing to scare you."

The four, feeling just a bit apprehensive, headed towards the entrance. The right hand door was open and they stepped inside, their shoes sounding loud on stone tiles. Signs which would direct people when the Hall opened were stacked on one side and a book to sign in was on a low table. Sarah signed them in, shepherding them towards another door, level with the main front of the house.

"Welcome to Tylluan!" she announced grandly as they all stepped into the main part of the building and had their first look inside. They had entered halfway along a great hall which stretched to their left and right towards internal dark panelled doors. A large grand reception hall, long and thin, it ran along the front of the building. Across the hall from them was a stone fireplace big enough for the children to stand inside.

James looked up. "Wow, just look at the work in the ceilings!" he whispered in awe, pointing to the elaborate plaster coving and roses that adorned edges of the pale ceiling and around the four large black candle filled chandeliers that hung down at regular intervals along the middle of the room.

Sarah was delighted at his appreciation, "They're beautiful aren't they. I did quite a bit of work on the features in this room. Electricity was brought in a long while after the Hall was built you understand, and they never wired it into this reception hall. When it's dark and the candles are lit and the fire burning it really is so atmospheric."

"I'll write about this place in a story," said Jenny, "This hall will be full of knights having won a battle."

It genuinely was a stunning room and they could have stayed, but Sarah hustled them left and through the door at the end of the room into a smaller room at the corner of the hall.

"This is the room I'm currently working in," she said, pointing up at the delicate decor she was painstakingly restoring, "so this is your base. I've packed lunch for us all, come for it when you fancy. I'll just quickly find Jake for you and then you can go exploring all you like."

The four looked at each other, smiling. To be left on their own to explore was going to be perfect. While Sarah disappeared to find Jake, the four held a conference.

"Right, what are we going to do?" asked Barrie.

"How do you mean, we're going to look round aren't we, see if we can solve the mystery." replied Jenny, looking confused.

"Yes, but we need a plan. How many people will have looked round here and failed to find anything? The staff here, the police, we need to think of the places they may have missed."

"We need to be methodical, like we were when searching for the key to the barn," added James, agreeing with Barrie. The key to the barn. It had only been two days ago, but seemed almost a lifetime, with everything that had gone on in-between.

"Why don't we look around first, then we will know what there is, and can plan from there how to search?" suggested Liz, who was dying to be off exploring, and they all agreed. They would have a good look round first, see what places Jake had to show them, and then decide where to hunt for the missing silver.

Sarah came back as they were finishing their discussion. Jake followed her, dressed in a green t-shirt with an open checked shirt over, and was whistling a tune as he walked.

"Hey," he said to the four, smiling broadly. "All set for a day's exploring? I've got a few bits I need to get on with now, before my cement goes off, so can I meet you at about," he paused to look at his phone for the time, "half past ten?"

"That would be great, thank you," said Barrie, and the others added their thanks.

"Great, I'll see you back here at half past ten then," and he was gone, jogging back through the main hall and out of sight.

"He is kind, giving up his time for us when he's obviously really busy," commented Jenny, as she watched his retreating back disappear.

"Very," agreed Barrie. "Shall we explore ourselves then for the next hour and a half, we surely can get this place looked over briefly in that time. Let's just have a look round together, then, if we need to, we can split up later to hunt in places." The others thought this was a great idea and they all set off bidding Sarah, already up a ladder, a cheery farewell.

Crossing back through the main entrance hall, the four entered the room at the far end, and found themselves in a grand lounge. It was richly decorated and sumptuous curtains hung around the tall windows. The wooden floor was highly polished and period furniture was placed carefully, giving the room a very spacious yet warm feeling. Dominating the room was, again, a large and gothic looking stone fireplace, with wooden panelling from floor to ceiling.

"It seems almost homely," commented Jenny, "I could just curl up in that large chair."

"We haven't time to be curling up!" said Liz, poking Jenny in her ribs. "Come on, we've secrets to explore and treasure to find!"

They crossed the room to another dark coloured door in the corner, heading into what seemed to be the centre of the Hall. A great staircase dominated the space, rising up towards the rear of the building, between two large wooden finials carved as owls, before dividing in two and curving back on itself as it disappeared out of sight.

"Whoa, isn't it grand," whispered Liz, putting her foot on the bottom stair and running her hand over the carved owl.

"Hang on," replied James, "I thought we were going to do this methodically, we've not finished looking downstairs yet. Let's finish there and head upstairs after."

"Okay," agreed Liz, stepping back, "Lead on!"

There were several other doors leading from the central stairway, James opted for one on the same side as the lounge, heading towards the rear of the hall. Through the door a short flight of steps lead down and along a short passageway to a large, stone flagged, kitchen, occupying the rear corner of the hall. A black cooking range dominated the room, taking up almost half of one side. The windows were high up on two sides, and let ample light fall onto a huge scrubbed pine table, which could have easily sat a dozen or more people round. There was a small room, which the four took to be a pantry and a scullery leading off from the kitchen. The scullery had a door which led outside, Barrie tried it, it was locked.

"We need to do inside first, anyway," said Jenny, and they headed back into the main part of the house, to explore the other half, and upstairs. Room after room they looked in, most appearing to be near completion. Notable, by its absence in a large second drawing room, was the silver.

Huge, velvet lined, display cases stood empty, reminding the four of their mission; to find the missing items. A lot had been taken, judging by the cases.

"We need to have it in our minds, as we go into every room, where any hiding places may be. If the silver hasn't been taken away, it's been hidden really well, so keep thinking about places," said James.

"I don't think we need to bother with places like cupboards and chests of drawers do we?" asked Barrie, and James considered this.

"No, those aren't really hiding places, and will have already been searched, I imagine. We need to look at places where adults won't have even thought of," he replied and led them to a door at the rear of the hall, the only place they hadn't explored downstairs.

"Gaa, I'm so excited," squeaked Liz gripping Jenny's arm tightly.

The door lead out to a large conservatory area, where Jake was working.

"Well, hello you, how are you getting on?" he asked, putting down a trowel and coming to them.

"It's amazing here, you and Sarah are so lucky to be able to work here every day. Makes me want to do this sort of thing when I'm old enough," replied Barrie.

"Well, I get to do lots of dull jobs being a builder, but you are right, I am lucky to be involved with this, it's a lovely grand place. Have you been upstairs yet? There are three staircases that lead upstairs, and find the hidden entrance to the cellars too. There, that should keep you busy. I'll be another hour here, this was the old greenhouse and we've turned it into a conservatory where visitors can have tea and cake. See there, we've installed visitor toilets, the old Hall plumbing couldn't have coped with a hundred bottoms a day." That made the four giggle with embarrassment, and Jake laughed at their faces.

"Come on then," said James, and they headed inside.

They sat for a conference at the foot of the great staircase. "We're not doing very well at finding places are we," said Barrie, and Jenny understood what he meant.

"No, if we've missed two staircases going up, and one going down, we haven't been looking all that well, and we have been trying. Let's look upstairs and see if we can find the top entrances to the stairs as we explore round."

They headed up the great staircase and went into room after room. Most had high ceilings and were impressively furnished with either four post or fancy cast iron beds, dark, highly-polished wardrobes, chests of drawers and cast iron fireplaces. There were two bathrooms, each with black and white tiled floors and large enamel baths. Liz was particularly taken with the highly decorated matching sinks and toilet bowls, and could see why Jake had said they wouldn't want hundreds of bottoms on them.

A spiral stone staircase led up from a corner of the landing to the tower, but, when the children got to the top of the stairs a locked door blocked their way and they could go no further. Returning down and going towards the rear of the hall, they took a narrow passageway up a couple of steps and came to what was clearly the servants' quarters. Everything here was plain and simple. Single cast iron beds, and functional furniture adorned each room, with a large jug and basin for washing in. No plumbing for the servants, thought Jenny as she peered in each room. They did, however have a fire in some of the rooms, but, as Jenny thought, that was probably out of necessity, for the winters would be cruelly cold up here in the high hills.

It was at the back of the servants' quarters that Liz, letting out a whoop of triumph, found one of the secret staircases. "Look, here! A staircase!" she cried and the others ran to where she called from. Sure enough, behind a screen in the corner of the passageway narrow stairs led down into darkness.

Liz was down them in an instant, and the others followed, bumping into the back of each other in their excitement. The stairs came out into the scullery, through what the children had thought was a cupboard door set into the wall.

"Stands to reason I guess," said James. "The staff aren't to be seen getting up and downstairs for an early breakfast before the family have theirs. But for the life of me, I can't imagine where the second one is. We've searched all round the place now."

The four headed back to the great staircase and sat at the middle landing.

"Well, what have we found for hiding places?" asked Barrie.

"I think the fireplaces are a good bet," suggested Jenny, and the others agreed. "There are so many, and most of the ones on the ground floor are big enough for one of two of us to stand in, we need to shine a torch up into them."

"Or the cellar," suggested Liz, who had been frowning hard in thought. She took from her pocket her paper bag of fizzy cola bottles. "Four left, who would like one?" she said, offering them round.

"Oh, thanks, said James, taking one. "I don't know how you've made them last so long," he said, before putting one into his mouth and wincing at how sour it was. "Cor, that's gone straight to my jaw!" he exclaimed, pulling a face and the

101

others laughed, all sucking busily on one each and making similar faces.

Liz screwed the paper bag into a ball and threw it up and down, catching it in alternate hands.

"Over here," called Barrie, holding his hand out, he loved a ball game, Liz threw the impromptu ball to him, and watched as her aim was way off the mark and the bag flew high up and over the banister to the floor below.

"Idiot," laughed Barrie, and got up to go and collect the bag. He aimed a mighty kick at the little bag, as he got to it, to kick it against the panelled wall, but as the others watched, his foot slipped on the tiled floor and down he crashed, sliding into the panel. The others jumped up.

"Are you ok?" shouted Liz, running down the stairs. "Heavens to Betsy, you've gone through the panel!"

Alarmed at the damage, the others all ran to where Barrie was picking himself up.

"It's ok!" said James. "You've found the stairway Bar, look!" They crowded to see and the panel Barrie had fallen against was, in fact, a hidden door.

Chapter Twelve

On the Hunt for the Silver

The four had investigated the secret staircase and had found, rather disappointingly, that it just led up to another hidden panel in a corner of the main landing. They had returned to the front of the hall and hadn't been waiting long when Jake arrived, whistling a tune, before smiling as he saw them. "Well, how have you found it so far?" he asked. "Did you find the staircases and the cellar entrance? Are you ready for looking in secret and special places the public won't have access to?"

"You bet!" chorused the children.

"We've found quite a few already I think," said Liz, who was quite taken with Jake. "We've been up the hidden servants' stairs, Bar tripped against the secret door that lead up to the landing, and we found the tiny staircase from the servants' quarters to the kitchen, but we haven't yet found the cellar entrance."

"Ah yes, it's a tricky one is that," said Jake, "but the public will have access to that, so it's not as special as where I can show you. Now, have you been up the stairs to the tower room?"

"We have, yes, but it was locked." replied Barrie, "Have you a key?"

"Have I a key? Have I a key?" repeated Jake, tapping each of his pockets in turn. He looked puzzled and then put his hand behind Liz's left ear, and appeared to draw from it a large iron door key!

Liz squealed in delight and the other three laughed. It was a very good trick, Jake certainly was a fun person to be around.

"You carry it," said Jake to Liz, holding the key out to her. "Let's go and show you the tower. It will be open to the public when it's finished of course, but I've another surprise for you when we're up there."

"Great," chimed James and Barrie together, and Jake led the way through the reception hall and the great drawing room. They followed him towards the rear of the Hall, up the stairs the four had climbed earlier that morning onto the first floor, then along the passageway to the winding set of stairs that led to the tower.

Up the stairs in single file they all went, Jake leading, with Liz following closely behind, clutching the precious key tightly in her hand. It was in fact longer than her hand and made of black iron. It must be hundreds of years old, she thought, turning it over and examining it as she climbed the stairs. They soon arrived at the locked oak door they'd previously seen, and Liz excitedly put the key into the large keyhole. Try as she might, she couldn't get the key to turn.

"We're jinxed with keys and locks," commented Jenny, as Jake took hold of the key and jiggled it in the lock.

"It's only a bit stiff," he said, "I'll pop a drop of oil in it later, we're working up here this afternoon." A couple clicks were heard and the door swung open.

"Oh wow!" exclaimed Liz as she passed through into the room. It was large and square, with huge windows on three sides, just like those at the front of the hall. Against the wall with no window was a grand four poster bed, made of mahogany that seemed to gleam like a newly opened conker. Aside from the great bed, the only other items in the room were a number of large tin buckets placed at various points across much of the floor.

"This room had a bit of a leak problem," explained Jake, seeing the children looking at the buckets. "Look up and you will see our next task."

Looking up, the four saw the badly damaged ceiling, with plaster hanging off in great sheets.

"Gosh, you've got a job there! Where do you begin?" asked James, who couldn't imagine how the ceiling would ever look as smart as it evidently had, judging by the decorative plasterwork round the edges.

"Well, we first had to repair all the leaks, the roof was damaged in so many parts above us that we ended up just re-roofing the whole of it. It isn't that large and would have taken longer to do so many patches. Besides, a lovely old place like this deserves a proper job doing. All the furniture from here was taken out, except the bed as it was too large, but everything had been covered in waterproof sheeting by the family years ago when the roof first started leaking, so it wasn't too badly damaged."

It was clear that Jake cared about his work and talked animatedly in detail about how they would then painstakingly restore the plaster and lath ceiling, using modern plaster. Picking up a piece that had fallen to the floor, he showed them the horse hair that was used in the original plaster and they all passed it round, looking at it with polite interest.

"What a view!" exclaimed Jenny excitedly from the window that looked out over the rear of the hall, across the manicured lawns, part of the lake to the trees that lined the river, marking its path as it flowed through the valley.

The other three crossed to her, picking their way between the buckets. They saw that some still contained a small amount of water from when the roof leaked, and all stared out at the view, as Jenny got out her phone to photograph it.

"We weren't that far from here yesterday in the kayaks, look," said Barrie, pointing to the curved line of trees.

"What?" snapped Jake, startling them. "What do you mean, in the kayaks?" The four felt quite alarmed by his tone, and James decided in an instant to play it down and not mention the passageway.

"Oh, we found some old kayaks in the barn at Bar's farm, and just paddled them down to his nain's, that's all. It wasn't very interesting," he added, looking pointedly at the other three in case any of them chose to volunteer any comments about the passageway they'd found.

"Blooming crazy if you ask me," continued Jake, "I didn't think your parents were so irresponsible Bar, that river is dangerous, you shouldn't be paddling on it. I shall tell them not to let you again."

"It, er wasn't anything special," said Barrie, his face flushing at the criticism of his parents. "We had all the safety gear and Nain was waiting for us at her place."

"So, how long will it take you to fix the ceiling?" asked James, desperately trying to change the subject.

"Oh, erm, a week or so. Sorry, I didn't mean to shout, I er, I was just worried about you, that's all. I'd hate to think of you getting hurt." In an instant Jake was back to his smiley happy self, explaining how they'd start on the ceiling that afternoon, and how they'd have it looking as good as the day it was first created, over two hundred years before.

"Anyway, everyone will be able to come into this room when it's open, let's take you a few places they'll not be allowed. I bet you didn't even notice the door at the top of the tower steps behind the curtain did you?" he crossed the room back towards the door, beckoning for the others to follow him. There was an almighty clang and a shriek as Liz, turning to follow Jake, put her foot straight into one of the buckets and tripped over, sending the other buckets flying as she sprawled on the floor. Jake and the other three raced to pick her up, as, shocked more than injured, Liz shed a few tears. The rim of the bucket had bashed her shin, but there was no blood.

"There, you're not much hurt. At least there was no water in that one, my fault, I should have moved them all out of the way," said Jake, picking her up and sitting her on the bed. "On a bed fit for a queen, you are. Here, this will make it all better." Reaching into his pocket he brought out a paper bag of boiled sweets and held the bag out to her. Wiping her tears Liz took an orange one, her favourite.

"Thank you" she said, sniffing and rubbing her shin. "I'm ok, it was just a bit of a shock, that's all." Jake offered the other three the sweets and they all took one before heading for the door.

"Come on, Liz," called James, over this shoulder, "we can't explore without you."

Liz hopped down from the bed and forgot her bruised shin as, just through the tower room door, Jake drew back a deep red velvet curtain that was hung along the wall, exposing a small arched oak door, like a smaller version of the front door.

"Now, you'll have to be careful, no running about. This leads onto the roof of the Hall. The views are amazing, and it's lovely to be up high in the fresh air, but there's only the low castellations to stop you pitching over the edge, so I'm really trusting you to be careful. Mind, I'd not bring you out here if I didn't think you would be sensible."

"We'll be really careful, we promise," said Barrie, and the others added their agreement.

Jake drew out another great old key from his pocket and unlocked the door. It swung outwards with a small creak and he stepped through onto the roof of Tylluan Hall.

The four all gingerly stepped onto the roof, amazed at the difference it made, being outside and up high, instead of trapped behind glass.

"Gosh," exclaimed James. "It makes me feel like I'm a bird up here, doesn't it feel so weird and kind of free."

"Yes, I feel I could fly," replied Jenny, spreading her arms out wide, mimicking the action of a bird.

"Well, don't you go trying. Fall like a stone you would!" said Jake, smiling as he gestured to the four. "Follow me, and we will walk all round the roof. No one will be allowed out here when the Hall is open, so you're four of very few to see these views. Careful mind, just stay behind me, don't go too close to the edge."

The four followed eagerly. Although the roof looked as if it would be flat, it was not at all, but a mass of odd pitches, gulleys and huge chimney stacks, dotted all about, each topped with several fancy chimney pots.

"There are just so many chimneys," commented Barrie, as he tried to count them.

"Well, there's one for each fire isn't there, Jake?" replied James.

"Yes, that's right, every room pretty much has a fire. All the bedrooms do, all the reception rooms, then there's the kitchen. All those stoves you saw, they were run on wood, and then coal fires. The sweep is coming at the end of the week to sweep out all the chimneys so that we might have the odd fire lit come the winter months - just to add to the feel of the place. Oil fired central heating was installed by the trust some years back, and that keeps out most of the cold."

Jake went on to tell them about how children were used in Victorian times to climb up inside the chimneys and brush the soot out by hand. He was so knowledgeable and interesting to listen to, his welsh accent adding almost a musical quality to his words, that the children could have listened to him for hours, stood up there in the glorious July sun. School and normality seemed a million miles away.

Jake pushed himself off the stack and they all continued round the roof, marvelling that they were seeing bits of the Hall no one else would get to see.

As they went round to the "East Wing" as Jake called it, the side furthest from Pen Y Bryn farm, Barrie's sharp eyes were drawn to a stone archway that seemed to lead down into the ground itself. It was close to the lake, though so hidden by overgrown climbers that it appeared, to the casual observer, to just be a curious mound in the ground.

"What's that Jake? Is that an archway I can see under the tangle of plants?" he asked, pointing to it. "It looks exciting."

"That's the old ice house," answered Jake, and walked on.

"An ice house? What's one of those?" asked Jenny, Liz thought she knew.

Jake paused and turned back, before settling himself against a chimney stack as the four gathered round.

"In the Victorian times ice was very expensive during the summer months. Those that could do so gathered, or bought in, great slabs of ice and stored them in their ice houses. The ice house needed to be near cold running water, ideally by an underground stream or lake, so the temperature was always low and the ice would last longer. That one runs down to the underground stream that feeds the lake. It's just some archways and a few underground rooms, nothing exciting." The four all felt a tingle go down their spines at Jake's description. How on earth could that be classed as not exciting? James voiced the question everyone wanted to ask, "Can you take us there next please, Jake?"

"I can't, no, it's shut off, it's all falling down see, so we've locked the gates."

"Ok, well, can we at least go with you and look from a safe bit, please?"

Jake's reaction was almost an explosion. "No! I cannot and will not take you there! It's far too dangerous! The roof is in poor repair, it all needs shoring up before anyone can go in, and even then it would be too dangerous for anyone that doesn't have to be there. Even we are not going in there before the experts have assessed it, so if it's too dangerous for me, it's definitely too dangerous for you. Honestly, first going down the river, then wanting to go in there, you kids seem absolutely determined to do yourselves harm. It's not a playground round here you know! End of discussion!"

"Okay, okay, I'm sorry, I didn't mean to upset you," said James, taking an involuntary step back at the unexpected anger his question had provoked. Liz had tears in her eyes and both Barrie and Jenny looked visibly shocked.

Jake looked at the four, and seemed awkward as he sought the right words.

"Hey, I didn't mean to upset you, sillies. It's just I don't want you hurt, see? You're good kids, I'd not want anything bad to happen, I didn't mean to upset you." He put his arm round Barrie, who was closest to him. "Come on, let me get you all some torches and I'll let you loose in the cellars, you can have a real treasure hunt down there. No one has been in them for ages, if the silver's anywhere, my bet would be it's there, if it's still here at all."

Jake was very animated, seemingly eager to make up for his outburst, and he chatted non-stop as he led the four from the roof, down the tower steps, and into the rear of the Hall, to a room where evidently the builders stored lots of tools.

"Just get you something from here, then I'll show you the door to the cellar and unlock it, then you can explore it to your heart's content after lunch."

"Thank you very much," said James, who was surprised looking at his watch to see that it was just beyond midday already. How the time had just flown.

"Right, let's see, here we are," he said, triumphantly holding up a rather moth-eaten head torch and a powerful LED hand torch. "Only the two I'm afraid so you will have to share, but you won't want to go round the cellars on your own anyway - rumour has it, they're haunted!"

Chapter Thirteen

Jenny's Discovery

Jake lead them back into the room with the main staircase and took them down the left hand side, walking under the upper half of the stairs. Turning, he grinned at them, inserted a key into a tiny keyhole, barely visible in the panelling on the side of the central staircase. There was a click, and the panel popped out slightly. It was another secret door! Jake pulled the door open and stepped inside, going underneath the stairs.

"See, there's the steps down to the cellar. There was also an entrance to it from outside I believe, but there's no sign of it now, so that will be for phase two of the restoration. For the time being, there's just this one entrance."

The four shivered, it looked very dark in the cellars, and cold too.

"If there's no other way in, and you have the key, how come you think the silver is down there?" asked Jenny, impressing the others with her shrewd questioning.

Jake paused, "Well, the key was only found last week, until that point it was open to anyone, so anyone hiding the silver could have, and now can't get to it. I locked it up until it can be searched properly, so you can be the first team to search."

This all made sense and sounded very exciting to the four.

"It's definitely a possibility!" said Barrie, his voice rising with excitement.

"Well, have your lunch and then you can astound us all with the treasure find," said Jake, leading them back out from under the stairs. "I'll leave the key in the lock, and will be either in the conservatory or tower room if you need me." The four headed back to the room where Sarah was still hard at work. On the way there they had a hurried conversation about Jake's outbursts, and all agreed not to mention anything in front of Sarah. They thought this was best in case it resulted in a change of heart about kayaking on the river, and meant they couldn't explore the passageway.

They ate a delicious picnic of sandwiches, fruit and crisps, each taking turns telling Sarah about the morning's adventures and the excitement of going up onto the roof and finding the hidden staircases. Sarah was delighted that they were enjoying the Hall as much as she did; she'd been a little concerned that they might have been bored after an hour. She showed them the work she'd been doing on the restoration, which was impressive and so painstakingly delicate that the children enthused greatly.

Excitedly, they told her of the afternoon plans to explore the cellars and then the fireplaces.

"You'll all be for baths when you get home then, you'll be as black as sweeps," Sarah laughed, adding that they'd need to put jumpers on to go into the cellars as they'd be cold.

The four all had brought them, so finished their lunch, put on their jumpers and eagerly headed back to the main staircase to explore the cellars.

James wore the head torch and Liz carried the hand held one. It was spooky descending the stone stairs into the darkness, with only the light of the two torches illuminating small areas.

"Sarah was right, it's cold down here," said Jenny, shivering, partly due to the temperature, partly due to the excitement. The shadows seemed to leap out at them, and cobwebs hung low from the ceiling, making Jenny shy away from them, she wasn't a fan of spiders. The cellars comprised of several rooms, with archways separating them.

"We need to search methodically again, like we did upstairs," said Barrie, who had high hopes of finding the silver in the cellars after what Jake had told them.

"It's not going to be easy, look at how many boxes and cases there are," added Liz, pointing over to stacks of tea chests.

"No, but it's our best shot, and we can manage it," Barrie replied, and they set to work.

Slowly and surely they made their way round the cellars, room by room. There were four in total, varying in size and shape. One was set out as a huge wine cellar with racks of old dusty wine bottles from floor to ceiling. Most were empty, and Liz spent a good deal of time carefully pulling out each bottle to check behind it for the silver.

"Three hundred and eighty six bottles, and not a drop of silver!" she exclaimed in frustration, as she put the last bottle carefully back into the rack.

"This might be something," called James, who was in a small cellar, the last one to be searched, with Jenny. Liz and Barrie rushed over to where his voice came from.

Coughing from the dust, James and Jenny emerged, James carrying a small metal box.

"It was hidden in a corner, behind a stack of empty tea chests," said Jenny.

"It isn't very old by the look of it, and someone obviously did not want it discovering," added James, "but I think it's locked." He passed the box to Barrie and they all clustered round it to see if it would open.

The box was like the cash box that was used at the tuck shop at Grey Owls Boarding School. It was quite small, but easily large enough to contain some, if not all of the silver.

"It's definitely locked, I can't open it," said Barrie, grimacing with the effort of trying to prise the lid.

"But why would you put something like a locked box, behind tea chests? Were they stacked up as if to hide it?" asked Liz and Jenny replied enthusiastically.

"Yes! Absolutely as if to hide it!"

James took the box back from Barrie, "Let's think about this, how heavy is it?" he mused, weighing the box in his hands. They all had a hold of the box and considered that, while it was not extremely heavy, neither were small items of silver, so it was possible that it could contain them.

"How frustrating that we can't get into it!" exclaimed Barrie.

"I guess we could ask Jake to help open the box," suggested James. "He did say to find him if we needed anything."

There was silence, as they all remembered Jake's uncharacteristic outbursts.

"I feel a little nervous of him now," said Jenny.

"Well, he said he was just concerned for our safety, and he was fine afterwards, showing us down here and getting the torches. Dad always says the world is 'Health and safety gone mad' so perhaps he's just, you know, conscious that we could be hurt." James was always keen to see the best in everyone. The girls mumbled their agreement as Barrie started towards the stone stairs that would take them back up to the hall.

"Come on!" he shouted. "We could be holding the treasure!"

They all clattered back up the stairs and emerged into the hall, blinking at the sudden bright daylight.

"You know we've been down there for over two hours!" said James, looking at his watch. "Didn't that time just fly?"

115

Jake wasn't in the conservatory, so they all ran up the staircase and then the spiral stairs to the tower room.

"Jake!" called Liz, breathless from the mad dash up the stairs. "We've found the treasure!"

"Shut up, we haven't, we don't know what's in the box," reproofed Barrie. Liz reddened and turned away

"We've found a box but we can't get into it," explained Barrie, holding the box out to Jake. "Do you think you would be able to get into it for us?"

Jake took the box, "So this might be the missing silver eh? Well, I tell you, if it is, I'll take you all out for burger and chips." He gently shook the box, there was definitely something in it, and he tried to prise it open, as Barrie had.

"I can cut the hinges and open it," Jake suggested, frowning at the box. "We have to find out what's inside!"

He was back to being his usual cheery self and the four all relaxed. He was as excited as they were about the box, and led the way from the tower room back down to the conservatory where several tool boxes lay open on the floor. Jake selected a small hacksaw and began working at the hinge of the box.

"I could just drill through the lock, but it would risk damaging whatever is inside," he explained as he sawed back and forth.

"Can I have a go please?" asked James, and Jake passed him the saw, helping him position it against the partially cut hinge.

"We should all cut a bit, team effort and all," said Jenny, and so they took it in turns, each cutting at a piece until as Barrie gave a triumphant grunt, the second hinge gave way.

Jake took the box back and began twisting the lid back and forth to get the lock to disengage. As soon as it was free, he held it out to the four, without opening it.

"Here, this is your adventure, you found it," he said, smiling broadly at them.

There was a clamour of excitement and, as James had found the box, they all decided he should get to lift the lid.

"Three, two, one," he lifted the lid away and five heads bent forward to look inside.

In the box was a folded brown envelope, and James picked it up.

"Doesn't feel like silver," he said, disappointedly tipping the envelope into the palm of his hand.

Out fell a collection of keys, all various sizes, but each one looking as old as the Hall.

"Ah fantastic!" burst Jake. "That's wonderful, that is! We've been missing most of the internal keys in this place, I bet these are they!"

The four, try as they might, could not match Jake's enthusiasm about the keys, having set their hearts on silver. Jake looked at their downcast faces. "Hey, don't look down, you've made my day with these, and the Hall can retain its original locks - that's a treasure in itself that is!"

They all felt a bit better hearing that, though Barrie was keen to get back to the treasure hunt.

"Well, we've done the cellars, so now we just have to look into every fireplace. Is it ok if we keep hold of the torches till we've done that, please, Jake?"

"Of course it is, and it's a good thought, searching there. You may be onto something." Jake really was so encouraging that as the four set off to search the fireplaces, they agreed heartily, that he had only been concerned for them before, and that he was to be trusted.

They headed to the main staircase to begin searching the fireplaces. There were over twenty in all, varying from small cast iron ones in the bedrooms to the huge stone ones downstairs that were big enough to stand in.

"We're going to be hard pushed to get all these done in the time we have left. Shall we split into pairs?" asked Barrie.

"We could," replied Liz.

"Any we don't get chance to search, you could always search yourself next week couldn't you, Bar? Or perhaps we could nip here on Saturday before we go, or even Friday if we have time?"

"That's no good," replied Barrie. "Don't you remember what Jake said? The chimney sweep is coming on Friday, so they'll find anything up there if we don't search it all now."

"You're right. That settles it," said James, looking determined. "We'll set to it now. Jen, you and I will search downstairs, Bar and Liz can search upstairs. Is that all right with everyone?" James never liked to appear bossy. The others all nodded in agreement and Barrie and Liz headed up the stairs to begin their search.

It was a dirty job and evidently the chimneys had not been swept for many years. Great sheets of soot fell down as the children poked about, causing them to cough and splutter violently.

"We're making a bit of a mess," said Jenny to James, looking with concern at the black footprints in the lounge hearth where they had just been searching. James went to the room Sarah was working in to get the dustpan and brush he had seen during lunch, while Jenny stood again in the lounge fireplace, shining the head torch up each side of the chimney. About half a meter up she saw an area to one side with a brick missing. Gingerly she put in her hand, but found just an empty void.

It took the children the rest of the afternoon to finish searching the fireplaces and kitchen stove. They met back up in the main stair hall and exclaimed at each other about the dirty mess they were in.

"Sarah should have us walking home, the state we're in," said James.

"That wouldn't be too bad," said Jenny. "Let's at least wash our hands and faces."

At that point they heard the tuneful whistle of Jake, coming down the stairs from the tower room. "My word!" he laughed, "I could cancel the sweep, looks like you've done the job for them! Come on, let's get you cleaned up, follow me out to the back."

They did and handed Jake the torches as he gave them some cleaner for their hands and faces, before digging out a soft brush he used when wallpapering. They all took their jumpers off so were at least presentable from the waist up and Jake showed them how to brush their jeans. Soon they looked pretty much unscathed and headed to find Sarah. Jake came with them, insisting on seeing them off, and commiserating with them about not finding the silver, but reiterating just what a fantastic find the keys were.

Sarah had ten minutes of work left and Jake helped tell the tale of the key find to her.

"Well, will I see you again this week?" he asked the four. They shook their heads sadly.

"Ah, that is a pity, it's been fun having you about." He paused. "Er, when it is you go home, you three?"

"Saturday," said Jenny, with an exaggerated sigh, throwing her arms in a dramatic gesture.

Sarah gathered up the picnic bags and Jake took them from her, insisting on helping her to the car with them and seeing them off.

The four followed, taking their last look at the Hall, whose mystery they had failed to solve.

Jake loaded the bags into the boot of the car. "Well, enjoy the rest of your stay, and remember what I said about the river." The children all said goodbye to him and Liz gave him a hug. Sarah started the car and Jake gave the children a last, cheery wave from the main door before heading back inside.

"He's really taken a shine to you four," said Sarah. "He's never helped me with my bags before," she laughed, and began to drive slowly towards the main gates.

"He's been very kind," said Liz, who'd fully recovered from her fright at his outbursts. "We had a great view from the roof and from the tower room. I wish now I'd taken some photos while we were up there."

"I can send you the ones I took, though I didn't even think of taking any from the roof," offered Jenny, putting her hand in her pocket for her phone. She opened her eyes wide and began tapping all her other pockets, increasingly frantically. "Oh, no!" she cried, "I've lost my phone!"

Sarah brought the car to a halt, still on the long drive. Jenny, panicking, was delving into pocket after pocket.

"You had it out in the tower room," said Barrie. "You were taking photos there. I didn't see you take any photos after."

"You didn't take any when you were with me," added James. Liz put in, "I think you left it in the tower room, when I fell over." She closed her eyes as she recalled the memory of her tumble in the bucket, "You had both your hands on me, so you must have put it down."

Jenny thought hard, looking concerned. Sarah slid the car into reverse and began to head back towards the hall. As she pulled up she said, "Jenny, you pop back up to the tower room and look there while we check the car. Bar, why don't you check where we had lunch in case it's dropped out there?"

There was a flurry of activity.

"Do you want to stick together?" Barrie asked Jenny, as they ran to the front door.

"No, it's ok, we'll be quicker if we split up. I'm making Sarah late enough already."

"Ok," said Barrie and headed through the front door, turning left.

It didn't take Barrie long to look round the room, there was nothing there that they had left. He returned to the main hall and debated whether to go up to the tower room. He decided not; Jenny would be, no doubt, on her way back by now. He paused in the main entrance porch to wait for her. He could see through the side windows in the porch that the search of the car was almost complete; the bags which had been taken from the boot and emptied out were now being loaded back in. There was nothing he could do to help there then.

He hung about waiting. Jenny was taking ages. Was something wrong? Perhaps the tower room was locked again and she had had to find Jake for the key. He waited, considering again what to do. Everyone was in the car now, Jenny really was taking a long time.

Barrie had just made up his mind to go and look for Jenny when he heard the sound of running footsteps from the lounge and she appeared, out of breath, looking flushed and excited.

"You've been a time! Have you found it?"

Jenny, too breathless to speak for a moment, held up her phone in a mute reply.

"Great, come on then," Barrie said, heading out of the Hall towards the car. Jenny put her hand on his arm.

"I saw," she panted, "I saw someone go into the ice house." Barrie looked at her in surprise and stopped in his tracks. "Are you sure? Who was it?" he asked.

Jenny looked at him, her face deadly serious. "It was Jake!"

Chapter Fourteen

Conference in the Night

"Come on you two, have you found it? You've been ages!" called a voice from the car, abruptly halting any further discussion about Jenny's discovery.

"Yes!" Jenny shouted back, opening the car door and holding out her phone triumphantly, "You were right, Liz, you clever thing. It was in the tower room."

Everyone was relieved.

"Take two," said Sarah, pleased that she wouldn't have a distraught child to cope with, and began to pull away from the Hall again.

Barrie, sat in the front, couldn't see Jenny desperately trying to let James and Liz know about her discovery. Sarah's bright chatter, asking them again about their afternoon, prevented any covert sharing of news, however. Jenny didn't want to share the find with adults until all the four knew about it and could decide what to do.

Arriving back at the farm, much to Jenny and Barrie's frustration, they could not get any time alone to chat. Liz and James could sense that something was up and looked at Jenny with quizzical faces.

Through dinner they all told Alan about their adventures at the Hall and how exciting it had been, both out on the roof and down in the cellars.

Alan listened attentively, and was very interested in the discovery of the keys.

"What is it with you four and keys?" he laughed and said they shouldn't be too disappointed not finding the silver, in his opinion, it was probably long gone.

They finished the meal and Barrie was just about to suggest Liz, Jenny, James and himself went for a walk outside when Alan disappeared into the front room and returned with Monopoly.

"I've been on my own all day. As lovely as Katie is, she isn't the best at conversation. How about a game of Monopoly? It was your mum's favourite, Bar."

It would have been rude to refuse and so they cleared the kitchen table, getting out the game while Sarah made them all mugs of hot chocolate.

Alan helped Liz with the rules as she hadn't played before and soon everyone had transformed into ruthless property tycoons. Sarah, who seemed to spend most of the time in jail, went and put Katie to bed.

Late into the evening they played, and time seemed to disappear. At half past nine, with Liz in the lead, owning all the railway stations and Mayfair, Alan suggested they declare her the winner and call it a night.

They all agreed that was a good idea, Jenny yawning loudly.

"Come on then you all. Bed time," said Alan, and followed them, up the creaking stairs. Sarah was still upstairs with Katie who'd been slow to settle and called goodnight to the four.

Washing and brushing their teeth in turn Jenny passed Barrie on the landing.

"You and James come to our room at midnight," she said quietly. Barrie nodded, he was desperate to know exactly what Jenny had seen from the tower room.

"Goodnight kids, sleep well" said Alan, appearing on the landing. They all said goodnight and went into their bedrooms.

Jenny and Liz spoke in hushed tones, but after a minute Alan tapped softly on their door.

"Sleepy time you two, or you'll never be up tomorrow," he said, and they fell silent, lying in the darkness waiting for the house to fall silent and midnight to come. Tired as they were, they were too excited to sleep and listened to the grandfather clock chime the hours and half hours. It seemed to take forever, but at long last the clock chimed 12 and there was a quiet tap at the girls' door as Barrie and James sidled in quickly, closing the door carefully behind them. They sat at the foot of the girls' beds, pulling the duvets over them and Jenny, clicking on her bedside light, began to tell her story.

"I went up to the tower room, and thought Jake might still be up there. The door was closed so I knocked. There was no reply, so I tried the handle. It wasn't locked, so I went inside. There was no one there. I went to the window and there, on the stone ledge, was my phone. I picked it up and was just turning to leave when, out of the corner of my eye, I caught a glimpse of movement from the window that looks out over the other side of the lake and the ice house."

There was the sound of a door opening and Jenny immediately stopped talking, the four looked at each other in alarm.

"Light off," hissed Barrie. "It'll show under the door." Jenny quickly clicked it off, plunging them all into darkness. The four stayed absolutely still, not daring to move for fear of making a noise that would bring whoever was about into the room.

Jenny was sure her heartbeat would be heard by everyone, and could feel it thudding in her chest.

Alan could be heard walking up and down the landing, speaking to Katie in hushed, soothing tones, trying to coax her back to sleep. The boys hoped he wouldn't go into their room and find them missing. He didn't, but continued walking up and down the landing, whispering to Katie, who gurgled back.

It was a good while after the grandfather clock struck half past twelve that Alan and Katie finally returned to their bedroom and silence returned to the house.

Cautiously Jenny turned her bedside light back on, after getting the all clear from Barrie who'd peeked out into the hall.

"Where was I?"

"Movement by the ice house," said James, who was desperate to hear more of Jenny's adventure.

"So, I caught movement out of the corner of my eye by the ice house," recapped Jenny. "I crossed to that window to get a better look and could see, plain as day, Jake unlocking the chain that secured the ice house gate shut. He looked really furtive, kept glancing about to left and right, I was worried he may look back over his shoulder and see me, but he didn't."

"Are you absolutely sure it was Jake?" asked Liz, who was upset to think that Jake, who she liked so much, could have lied to them.

"Well, he was wearing the same clothes. At least, I think it was him. He had his back to me, unwrapping the chain, but it did seem to be him. That's why I was so long. I waited and waited to see him come out so I could get a look at his face, but he didn't. I started to think you'd be getting anxious to go, so I came away."

"So you're not positive it was him?" put in Liz, hopefully.

"It was him. I'm, er, 90% sure," said Jenny, though she sounded less certain that she had earlier. "Ah!" she exclaimed in a hushed tone of remembering. "I took a photo of the back of him, with my phone, let's have a look and see what we all think."

She brought out her phone and they all crowded round as she opened the photo gallery app and enlarged the photo.

There, in the middle of the screen was the figure of a man, dressed in blue jeans and an olive green t-shirt.

"His hair is the same, and that's what Jake had on, all right," said James, peering closely at the image.

"No, Jake was wearing a shirt." replied Liz, somewhat defensively.

"Yes, but under that was a green T shirt, his shirt was open when he met us, I remember it clearly," said James, who'd been taught by his father to notice what people wore and always did it as a little game with himself. Jenny flicked to another photo, showing the ice house gate open.

"I didn't dare take any more in case Jake saw me as he shut it," explained Jenny, "I stepped back, but he fastened the gate shut, and disappeared down into the ice house."

"I don't like this. I don't like this at all," said Barrie, in a very serious tone. "Jake is definitely up to something. Look at the way he flew off the handle about the ice house. On and on he went, saying how dangerous it was, too dangerous even for him, and here he is, going into it without so much as a hard hat."

"Perhaps the hard hats are inside?" suggested Liz, her voice trailing off under the hard gazes of the others.

"Don't be silly, besides, Jake said it was too dangerous for them even to go in to. A hard hat is hardly going to protect you if the whole roof caves in. No. I'm with you, Bar, I think there's a bit more to Jake than meets the eye," said James, looking very grown up and frowning deeply. "I wonder if I should speak to Dad."

"Oh no," put in Jenny, "let's see what we can find out first. After all, what would we tell him, Jake wouldn't let us go into the ice house but went in himself? For all we know there could be a perfectly simple explanation to it all and we'd be left looking like idiots."

The four discussed it further and all agreed that they should look into things themselves. Plans were made to ask to paddle on the river in the morning, so that they could perhaps moor up near the Hall and clamber up the bank to sneak to the ice house and see if they could see anything. It was gone half past one by the time the boys snuck quietly back to their bedroom and the four tried to get some sleep. They were all sure that they'd never manage to drop off with the excitement of Jenny's discovery and the questions going round in their heads. Was it Jake sneaking into the ice house? Why had he told them it was too dangerous to go in, only to then go in himself? What was his reason for keeping the ice house to himself? None of the four could answer the questions, but they all knew one thing; something was not right, and they would try their best to work out what Jake's secret was.

Chapter Fifteen

Downpour

What a different day greeted the four children when they, rather sleepily, went down into the kitchen for breakfast in the morning. Rain ran down the farmhouse windows and looked, according to Alan, "Set in for the day."

"I was awake during the night, I heard the clock chime four, it was already raining then," added Barrie, looking gloomy.

"Just as we had hoped to go on an all day picnic on the river."

"It's a real cloudburst, but it might clear," suggested Jenny, who, like the others, couldn't bear to think of their midnight plans spoiled.

James, his brow creased into a frown was looking at his phone.

"Not according to the forecast I'm afraid." There was a chorus of groans from the other three, slumping into their chairs around the table.

"There'll be plenty for you to do, don't worry," said Sarah, trying to cheer them up. "Alan's going to town this afternoon if you'd like to have a walk round there with him, and there's always the barns to explore more, here."

"Yes, it will be fine," smiled back James, who never liked to be an inconvenience.

The others all muttered polite acknowledgements and agreed, that it would all be ok. They couldn't help but feel frustrated though, all that exploring to do on the river and at Tully Hall, and no way of doing it.

"Can you please sort my new phone out, James? You did say you would this week, and it's nearly the end."

"Sorry, Liz, yes, no problem. I'll transfer it across today," replied James, and Liz beamed at him.

"You're the best! Thank you."

"I'll be clearing out more of the byre this morning, if you'd like to lend a hand," said Alan, as they all tucked into cereal and toast.

All four were keen to help and explore the byre. They changed into "scruffs" as Sarah called them; clothes that wouldn't spoil if they got a bit grubby, and headed into the byre, running across the yard so as not to get too wet.

It was an enjoyable morning, clearing out the old stalls. They were full of old, broken pieces of furniture, vintage farm machinery and timber. Alan explained how he planned to convert the byre into accommodation, so Sarah could offer bed and breakfast.

"Her cooking would be a treat for anyone," said James, who was always very complimentary about Sarah's meals. "I can't remember the last time I ate so well," he added, taking hold of an old plough with Alan.

"You getting the barn opened up has really helped me with this," said Alan, pulling the plough clear. "I've cleared a spot in there and we can store all the machinery and implements until such time as I can sort them out properly.

"Nain says you'll never sort the barn out, she said Taid never threw anything away if he thought it could be fixed," said Barrie, lending a hand to pull the plough.

The three strained with the effort of moving the heavy equipment.

"That's real horsepower for you," said Alan. "Well, I think he was right not to, Bar. Today's throwaway society causes so much waste and rubbish. Look at all the plastic rubbish there is in the sea, it wasn't a problem in your taid's day."

Barrie at once told his dad all about James' ability to repair peoples' phones and electronics, and how that saved waste. James blushed, but he looked pleased.

"Speaking of phones," called Liz from the other end of the byre where she and Jenny were wrestling a rotten table out to a bonfire heap.

"I'll do it tonight, I promise," shouted back James, and Liz smiled her thanks.

The rain did little to dampen the spirits of the four. It was impossible not to be jolly with Barrie's dad, and Sarah brought them all warm cups of tea and Nain's homemade brownies for elevenses, which were received with much enthusiasm.

At midday Alan declared that they'd done enough work for the day, joking that he didn't want reporting for child labour, and sent them inside to wash for lunch. A delicious selection of homemade sandwiches awaited the four and they tucked in heartily, having built up quite an appetite working in the byre. Sarah listened about all they had discovered and produced a surprise of Eton mess for pudding, as a treat for all their hard work. It was magnificent and James declared he'd happily live and work there every day if he would get paid in Eton mess.

"Your teeth would all fall out!" said Alan, laughing as all the children, looking mildly alarmed, began tapping at their teeth. "Well, I'm going into town this afternoon, I know you wanted to come, Liz, to send your parents a postcard. Does anyone else what to come?"

A chorus of "Yes please," rose at once from all the children and so, after clearing away the lunch things, the four piled into Alan's car and began the journey to the nearest town. It took a good half an hour to get to the little town. The rain had not let up at all and Jenny wondered out loud how the clouds could possibly have any left.

"We should buy an ark," suggested Liz, and Alan laughed. "It's not quite as bad as all that," he said. "It'll likely be fine again tomorrow."

"I hope so," replied Liz, "I do so hope so."

Alan, not knowing quite how badly the four wanted the weather to improve, gave Liz a reassuring smile in the rear view mirror and continued on.

It was a little after half past one when they arrived in the town. Barrie, keen to avoid any questions that his father might ask about why they all needed torches, suggested to him that he'd like to show the three round the town himself, and Alan agreed.

"I'll meet you back here at half past four," Alan said, "That should give you plenty of time for exploring."

They all thanked him and disappeared from his view down narrow, winding streets.

Taking them to a little hardware store, Barrie showed them a selection of torches.

"I'd quite like a head torch, like Jake had," said Barrie. "It would be useful for at least one of us to be able to have both hands free."

"You'd better lead the way if we're allowed to go tomorrow then," said James, selecting a small, but powerful, hand torch for himself. Jenny and Liz each picked up a purple LED torch and they went to the counter to pay for them.

"Off exploring are you?" said the shopkeeper, smiling as he put them in a bag. The girls reddened immediately, how could he know?

"Something like that," said Barrie, evasively, and thanked the man.

They wandered around the little town, dodging the rain showers. Jenny, James and Liz all bought postcards and Barrie, using the last of his savings, bought a small pair of binoculars.

"If we're going to do a bit of spying, these will make it much easier," he said, adding them to the torches in his bag.

Barrie next took them to a small cafe where, over mugs of hot chocolate, they wrote the cards, before heading to the post office.

"Have we got all we need, do you think?" asked Jenny, already imagining navigating down the passageway the following day.

"I think so," replied Barrie. "We have torches for the tunnel, there's rope for tying the kayaks to the bank, and binoculars for keeping watch."

"Explorers always have a compass," said Liz, "I wonder if there's an app."

James groaned dramatically. "Your poor phone will be filled with junk, just like your last one, I can almost hear it scream in protest."

Liz giggled, promising to be more selective.

It was soon half past four and, walking back towards the car park, they bumped into Alan on the way.

"What have you got there then?"

"It's, er, a secret," said Barrie, unable to think of a quick explanation and not wishing to lie to his father. Alan, who had a birthday the following month, decided it may be a gift for that, and asked no more questions.

They headed back, soon leaving the town behind and climbing up into the mountains.

Arriving at Pen Y Bryn Barrie gave a cry of delight. Nain's car was parked in the yard. He really was very close to her, and the other three children had taken to her at once, so were also happy. They raced in to see her, Barrie quickly handing the bag of shopping to James, who slipped upstairs with it before joining everyone in the kitchen.

Nain was on fine form and asked at once, how they had enjoyed the hall the previous day. The four took it in turns to tell the tale of finding the secret stairs and Nain listened appreciatively.

"Many a time I have been up and down those stairs when I was a girl," she said, and began to tell the four about life as a servant, having started work there at fourteen, not much older than they were now, as James pointed out.

"I don't feel old enough to start work now," said Liz, who, despite reassurance from the other three, often felt a little bit under confident.

"I don't think any of us do," said Barrie reassuringly.

"They were different times back then," reminisced Nain. "We had to grow up a lot sooner. I'm glad you can have a proper childhood. Don't you be in too much of a hurry to leave it. It is a wonderful time in your life. No, we worked hard from fourteen onwards. I'd have to be there for six o'clock in the morning. In winter, I would sleep in the servants' quarters when heavy snow was forecast. I'd to be bright and shiny as a new pin every day. Not a speck of dirt on me, or my pinafore, which, when you spend all day fetching, carrying, cleaning, scrubbing floors, washing, as well as clearing and laying the fires, is a task easier said than done."

"Did you ever go down into the ice house?" asked Barrie and the others pricked up their ears.

"Goodness me, I'd almost forgotten about that," said Nain, closing her eyes as she remembered back. "I didn't go there often, as it was deemed man's work, chipping the ice blocks up, but I did go and help Mr Soames, the butler, to carry the chips back sometimes. A cold, dark place is all I remember about it really. Did you go there?"

Barrie replied that they hadn't, being careful not to mention either Jake's outburst, or Jenny's subsequent discovery. He pressed a foot against Liz's leg, just to warn her not to say anything.

"It's in quite a bad state now, sadly," said Sarah, as she served up dinner for them all. "Jake searched it for the silver when we first heard of it missing, but was so worried about the condition, he condemned it and won't let anyone in, not even the other workmen he has with him. He quoted all sorts of health and safety legislation and padlocked it up. I don't know if it will ever be safe enough for people to go in."

The four exchanged knowing glances. Not safe enough for anyone to go in? They knew different.

The meal was, as usual, a happy one. Alan told Nain how the byre clear out was progressing, and they all enjoyed as she recounted back tales of when the byre had been full of cattle. Including when Bronwyn, a favourite milk cow, had managed to open the door and followed Nain's father, driving the horse and cart carrying the milk delivery, all the way to the Hall before he noticed. She'd stood calmly, munching grass on the lawn in front of the house, while he delivered the milk round the back to the kitchen. When he'd returned to the front, the whole family of the Hall were gathered round her, asking if milk was on draft that day. The four laughed loudly, they could just imagine it.

Conversation turned to what the children planned to do for their last day. Barrie described the picnic on the riverbank they hoped to have, if the weather improved. Nain looked a little concerned.

"Were you planning on having it at mine on the landing stage? Only, I'll not be there between midday and four, I'm in town myself tomorrow for a hairdresser's appointment. I guess I could cancel," she added.

"No Nain, you go. We were going to moor further upstream and ramble in the fields up there," said Barrie, considering it was close enough to the truth to not really be lying.

"Well, if you're absolutely sure?"

They were, and everyone crossed their fingers for a sunny day.

Dinner was finished and cleared away. Nain suggested the four have dinner at hers following their paddle the next day and promised to bake enough tasty treats to satisfy even the largest of appetites. It all sounded delicious and Sarah and Alan agreed that it would be a lovely way for them to end the week.

Liz brought her phones down and James began to transfer data from her old to new phone.

"I wouldn't know where to begin," said Nain, watching in admiration as James, quickly and deftly tapped the screens of the phones. "It really is like magic."

James continued into the evening with Liz's phone, spending time showing her how the different functions and features worked. Nain left for home and, as darkness fell, Alan declared it was time for bed.

"If you're paddling tomorrow, you'll need a good night's sleep, Jenny's yawning already."

There were no protests as they all wanted to have a quick discussion about the next day, so headed up the wooden stairs.

"I'll finish the last few bits tomorrow," said James, handing Liz both her phones, "or you can, just your files to go through, decide what you want to keep."

Liz thanked him and, with Jenny, went into their bedroom. It wasn't long before they were changed for bed and the boys popped in for a chat.

"Just checked the forecast on my phone," said James. "It is sunny."

"Great," chorused the others

Just got to hope we're allowed on the river," said Barrie.

"Well, if not, we just have to get back to Tully Hall. We must somehow get into that ice house," said James. Barrie, thought for a moment.

"So, if allowed on the river, we explore the passageway, then moor the kayaks up on the bank as close to Tylluan Hall as we can, scramble up the bank and then spy on the goings on in the ice house. If not, we return to the Hall, and try and keep an eye on Jake and the ice house. Agreed?"

"Agreed!" said everyone

"We MUST solve the mystery," said Jenny, raising her voice in desperation.

"Sshh. You'll bring dad up," said Barrie, handing her and Liz their torches. "We'll all get to bed. Last night was late and tomorrow, we will need all our brains to be on top form. One way or another, we're going to get into the ice house."

Chapter Sixteen

Back on the River

The sun was already streaming through the bedroom windows and, opening them, Jenny declared that the world had been washed and everywhere looked bright and vibrant. There was a tapping at the door and Barrie and James came in, full of energy.

"I think we'll be ok to go on the river," said Barrie, "It's a glorious day."

"What about what your dad said about the river flowing fast. Will that make them stop us going do you think?" asked Liz, looking concerned.

"I don't think it will too much," answered Barrie, looking at James, who considered.

"No, I think you're right. It's bound to make it flow a little faster, but we're pretty close to the source of it, the start of the river, here, so there's not as much water entering it as there is further down. It will be a lot more dramatic down river I imagine, but even that will be a few days away, the water needs time to drain down the mountains, so we should be ok."

"I nominate you to speak to Dad then, if he is worried," said Barrie, and James grinned.

"We'll dress for the river then," said Jenny, putting a pair of jeans to one side and selecting a pair of blue cargo style trousers. "I'm so excited, I really hope we get to go. It's our last chance of solving the Mystery of Tully Hall!" Jenny emphasised the last four words with her hands, as if it were a headline.

"We won't solve anything unless we get dressed and out," said Liz, still wearing her pyjamas. "Buzz off boys, we will see you downstairs. Work your magic James, so we're allowed to paddle."

When, ten minutes later, the girls arrived in the kitchen, both James and Barrie were smiling.

"Dad's going to have a look at the flow, but he thinks it'll be ok," said Barrie, in response to the girls' questioning expressions. Jenny and Liz visibly relaxed and breakfast was a very jolly occasion.

"I never knew a picnic could be so exciting," laughed Alan, and the four exchanged looks.

"It's not just the picnic," said Liz, and the other three stared at her, surely Liz wasn't going to tell them about the passageway. "It's the whole paddling on our own, tying up, clambering up the bank, finding the best spot," she drew breath as if to carry on listing.

"I know, I know," laughed Alan, enjoying hearing her excitement, "I'm just pulling your leg."

Sarah, who had been busily preparing sandwiches and wrapping slices of Nain's homemade brownies, turned around to the table.

"It will build you up a good appetite, so there's plenty of food made for you. Pick what drinks you would like to take and we will get you all packed up."

There was much toing and froing as the four got everything neatly packed into two sturdy bags, tying the tops of them tightly to try and make them waterproof.

"You don't want soggy sandwiches!" giggled Sarah and they all laughed.

As they all crossed the yard to get the kayaks from the barn, James whispered to Jenny,

"Torches, have you got yours?"

"Oh heck, no! They're by our beds," exclaimed Jenny in a frustrated whisper, before loudly gabbling something and running back to the farmhouse.

She soon returned, patting her pocket when she caught James' eye. They all put their buoyancy jackets and helmets on then, with Alan's help, carried the kayaks down to the river. Barrie had a large coil of rope over his shoulder and, as the kayaks were set down on the bank, fastened a length to the front of each one.

Alan looked at the water, "There's more water, clearly, and it's flowing a bit faster, but I'm happy to let you go. You have your phones on you?" They all replied that they had. "Good kids, I'm trusting you all to be careful and sensible. Please do not let me down. If paddling back up stream is too difficult after lunch, paddle down to Bar's nain's and call me, I'll collect you from there. Do not go any further down river than there, under any circumstances and be home by three o'clock. If you have any problems, any at all, phone me. I'll have my mobile on me, and Sarah would hear the house phone, so be careful, be safe, be happy."

"We won't let you down, Sir," said James, solemnly, recognising the speech by Alan as a portrayal of him feeling a little nervous about their trip, "I promise."

"Don't worry Dad, we'll be fine. We will find the best picnic spot, and you and I can go there next week."

"I will worry, it's what dads do, but that sounds great, Bar, I'll look forward to it."

141

"We will be careful, we're pretty sensible," added Jenny, just as Liz made her eyes cross and tapped herself on the head as if to free them.

"Oh, yes we are," Liz put in, looking a little embarrassed.

"I know you all are. I'd not have let you go otherwise."

Alan held each kayak steady as the four got in, Barrie and James sat in the front seats, with Jenny sat behind James, and Liz climbing in behind Barrie. They stowed the food away safely and got themselves comfortable.

"Are you ready?" With nodding of heads, Alan let go of the kayaks and the four began to paddle downstream.

"No later than three, remember!" he called and received a chorus of acknowledgements.

"Hurrah!" whooped Jenny, "We're off on an adventure! This has been the best week of my entire life. I've never had so much fun!" The others agreed.

The two boats drifted side by side, with only gentle paddling required from the children as the current carried them down the river.

"I vote we paddle to the Hall, and explore what's up that passage. It might well be nothing, in which case we can moor the boats somewhere close to that area and scramble up the bank into the grounds of Tully Hall. Then we can creep over to the ice house and see if we can find anything out. We can have our picnic after, how does that sound?" asked James.

"That's fine by me, good idea," said Barrie, and Jenny added, "We could, before going to the ice house, have a spy on it, keep it under sur, sur…"

"Surveillance" finished James, "Yes, great idea, we shall Keep Obs, as Dad says, and not show our hand. It we're spotted, it's game over as far as finding out about the ice house and I'd hate to be caught and end up in trouble with your parents, Bar."

"I don't see how picnicking would get us into trouble," said Barrie, "it is after all, what we said we were doing."

"If we were caught snooping, I bet we would end up in bother with Jake," said Jenny.

Liz, who'd been sat quietly paddling, exploded, "Oh I wish you would stop suspecting him of being bad. I'm sure there's a simple explanation for it all."

"Well, simple or not, I don't trust him and I'd love to find out exactly what he's up to," said James, sounding very serious and grown up. Liz looked mutinous.

They continued paddling. From the hills on both sides, water flowed down the steep narrow rocky stream beds, falling into to the river like miniature waterfalls.

"You can really feel the difference since Tuesday," commented Liz, trying to make up for her outburst, "I'm barely having to paddle at all."

"That's because I'm doing all the work!" retorted Barrie, laughing and Liz playfully splashed him with her paddle.

Rounding the bend in the river, the passageway in the wall was there on the left before they knew it.

"There's nothing to get hold of to stop ourselves!" shouted Barrie, as both kayaks passed the entrance.

"Back paddle! Back paddle!" shouted James, "Like Andy showed us! Quickly!"

It was panic for a few minutes as the four, somewhat clumsily, brought each boat to a halt and began the challenging task of paddling back, against the flow.

"This really is hard work," panted Barrie

"Yes, good job we are only a short way past the entrance. I don't fancy paddling all the way back," said Jenny, straining hard to pull her paddle through the water.

"No. Good idea of your dad's, Bar, to pick us up from your nain's," said James.

"Yes, I think we should do that," said Barrie, reaching the entrance to the passageway.

With a lot of bumping and scraping, against the brick walls, Barrie's and Liz's kayak nosed into the passageway. Liz had leaned back and taken hold of the rope at the front of James and Jenny's kayak, helping to guide it into the passageway behind them.

"Hang on. I can't see a thing." said Barrie, fishing in his pocket for his head torch. Fastening it around his helmet, he clicked it on and the passageway was instantly transformed from total darkness to a narrow, red bricked tunnel, with a curved roof about five feet above the water.

"There's no room to paddle, lie them in the kayaks and we'll use our hands to grab onto the brick wall and pull ourselves along."

"What can you see?" called Jenny, from the back.

"It continues on for quite a way. I think I can see a bend ahead. Definitely looks to lead somewhere, we will have to get further along."

Gripping as best as they could to the damp walls, the four inched up the passage, their minds racing as to where it might lead.

"It's curving to the left," called Barrie, as his kayak caught up on the wall and jammed fast against it. "We will have to wiggle round it, I think it should go. James, can you reach the rear point of our kayak and try and pull it a bit to the right? Maybe jam the front of yours down the left side?" James did as Barrie suggested and, grating along the wall, the kayak slowly came free. Liz pulled hard on the rope at the front of James and Jenny's kayak and, slowly, that too made it safely round the bend.

After a short distance Barrie called that the passage was opening up, the roof of the passage was higher by a few feet and it was now wide enough to paddle and easily turn the kayaks round. To their right was a stone walkway, just above the waterline. It was about twelve feet long and four feet deep, making a landing stage. The brick wall continued round it to the far corner where a wrought iron gate stood, through which the four, by the light of Barrie's head torch, could see a passage continuing. Upstream the roof descended steeply, to only a foot above the water, preventing any further travel by boat.

"Well, it looks like through that gate is the only way to go," said Barrie, scanning all round with his head torch. James had put his torch on, and also shone it round the area.

"It's like a manmade cave! Gosh, this is exciting!"

Barrie's torch light fell on the stone floor, fastened into the stone were large iron rings.

"Look! Mooring points! This place must have been used to bring stuff to in the past. Let's tie up so we can properly explore."

They nosed the kayaks to the rings and threaded the rope through, tying good strong knots so the boats would be safe and secure.

"Good idea of yours, Bar, tying the rope to the front of our boats before we set off," said Liz.

Barrie, climbing gingerly out onto the stone slabs, turned to help the others. "Well, are we all up for some exploring?" he asked, his eyes shining brightly with excitement in the dim light.

"You bet!" replied the others, the girls clicking on their torches.

"Just hope the gate isn't locked," said Jenny, shining her torch at it. "Have you noticed how similar it looks to the one at the entrance to the ice house? The one that was chained up."

"You're right," agreed James, "I wonder if we are near there?" He shone his torch up to the roof of the little cave. "It looks ok here, but let's be very careful, just in case it's falling in. We'll keep our helmets on."

The gate was not locked, and opened surprisingly easily, with only a slight squeak at the hinge. The four tiptoed through, talking in whispers. They followed the passage round sharply to the left, where it opened out into a large underground vault, with several stone arches, seemingly leading to smaller vaults. Another wrought iron gate stood, open at the far end and a passage led off, from which the smallest glimmer of daylight could be seen. James put a hand on Jenny's shoulder. "You were right, Jen, I believe we are in the ice house. Wait everyone, let's just have a look at the roof before we go any further."

Four beams of torchlight shone up at the roof of the vault. "It's beautiful!, Arched like you see in churches and in vaults beneath them," whispered Liz, "I can't see anywhere that looks to be falling down, it, well it looks pristine." Her voice trailed off as she came to realise the others may be right about Jake.

"I think we are safe to continue," said Barrie quietly, stepping forward. "Quite why Jake feels the need to keep this a secret I don't know."

"Can you hear that noise?" asked James, "I think the water runs right under the vault. That would explain why the roof of the waterway dropped down so low. What a feat of engineering, it really makes it feel cold in here."

147

The hairs on all the children's arms and back of their necks were standing up, but whether that was from the cold, or from excitement at what lay ahead, they could not tell. Quietly they moved forward, their torches shining on the entrance to the nearest vault.

"This must be where the ice blocks were stored," said Barrie as his torch illuminated the area inside the vault. It was about eight feet square, completely bare but for a stone slab at one end. They crossed the main vault to an archway opposite, leading to a second vault, identical to the first, but, although there was no ice to be seen, this vault was not empty. Wooden crates were stood along the side, filled with straw. "What's this about?" whispered Barrie, in surprise, and the other three entered the small vault behind him.

"Look at those," said Jenny, pointing to a corner where a pile of blue waterproof bags lay. "They are just like the ones we saw on Monday at the outward bounds place. What use are they here?"

"I have no idea," said Barrie, crossing towards the crates, "But aren't these like the ones we saw at the Hall, where Sarah was working? The packing crates items were stored in during the restoration?"

"Yes! They are!" said Liz, her voice rising in excitement. "What do you think is inside them?"

"I bet I know," said James, dropping to his knees by the crates. "Guys, I reckon we have found the stolen silver!" There were squeals from the girls.

Barrie, his arm already rummaging under the straw in one of the crates, whispered

"I've got something," and slowly drew out his hand, in which was grasped something small, but shiny.

Opening his hand, in the light of the four torches, there, lying in his palm, was a fine silver snuff box, with a coat of arms clearly engraved on the lid. The four gasped.

"The silver! The silver! I recognise the coat of arms!" cried Liz, her words tumbling over themselves in the exhilaration. There were whoops of joy from all four, as they hugged each other. What a find! Who would have thought they would actually find the missing silver. What would everyone say? A loud clang of metal on metal suddenly rang out.

"Shh!" hissed James, and the four, falling silent immediately listened.

"Sounds like a chain being moved. I bet it's the entrance gate being opened. Quick, what do we do?" whispered Jenny, feeling almost paralysed by fear.

"Have we time to make it to the boats and away?" whispered Barrie

"I don't think so," replied James, "We can try and hide in the first vault, the empty one. Come on, hurry."

Footsteps could be heard descending down the steps into the ice house and torch light bounced off the wall of the entrance passageway.

"Quick! In here!"

All four, as quietly as they could, dashed across the main vault to the first one they'd looked in. The girls and James were inside, but just as Barrie was at the stone arch entrance, torchlight fell straight on him.

"Stop right there!" said a familiar voice, but without any of its charm from before.

Almost frozen in fear, Barrie turned to face the voice. There, stood at the bottom of the entrance passage, looking even more thunderous than Mr Storm of Grey Owls could ever manage, was Jake. The four were trapped.

Chapter Seventeen

Prisoners Underground

Petrified, the four stood, frozen to the ground. Was it really their Jake and was he really as angry as he sounded? The other three turned round and saw it to be true. Jake stood, motionless and open mouthed, his face a mixture of fury and surprise.

"Hello Jake!" said Liz, smiling, even though she felt scared stiff. "How are you?"

Jake ignored her, instead clenching his jaw and fists as he thought quickly what to do.

"I thought I told you not to come down here," he growled

"We came up the water way," said Barrie, defensively, "How were we to know where it would lead to?"

"You shouldn't be here. No one should, it's not safe," said Jake

"Er, you're right. We are sorry, we'll go straight away, back down the water way and continue on our picnic. Ever so sorry for having surprised you," said Jenny, talking loudly and quickly, aiming to get as far away from Jake as possible. The others agreed in light and airy tones, realising at once what Jenny was trying to do.

"So sorry. We wouldn't have come here had we known," said James. "We'll be off." Edging to the front and turning to go down the passage to where they had left the kayaks.

Jake made a grunt as if to acknowledge their apology and send them away, so the four, acting as calmly and casually as they could, all started towards the tunnel through which they had entered the vault.

"Come on," whispered back James, leading the way, and Barrie, bringing up the rear pushed the two girls on.

"Act calm," he began when Jake's shout interrupted them. "STOP!"

Jake's voice boomed out and echoed around the vault, Liz gave an involuntary cry of alarm and Barrie, turning around, saw why Jake had shouted. He had crossed to the vault where the silver was hidden and could see, from the straw scattered on the floor, that the children had been to the crates and would know the silver was down there.

"So, you just couldn't keep your meddling noses out of it, could you? You just had to spoil things. Well, you're not spoiling things for me, see. Months I've worked here, and for what, a few quid. I was only taking what is owed to me."

The four listened in shock at Jake's attempt to excuse his behaviour.

"Tide me over a good while, the money from that silver would. Will," he corrected himself, "More use than being in a cabinet. It's mine and no one, I mean no one is going to stop me taking it."

"Jake, you can't," began James, but Jake cut him off.

"And what would you know?" he spat. "No, I've just got to work out what to do with you four."

There was silence while Jake considered what to do. The four, all now back at the entrance to the main vault, exchanged nervous glances. Liz took hold of Barrie's hand and he squeezed it back comfortingly.

"It's ok," he whispered, trying to remain calm and reassure her, although inside he was as frightened as she was.

"Right. You lot are just going to have to stay here. I can't have you telling anyone. You'll just have to stay put."

"But we will be missed!" said Jenny. "Everyone will be panicking and looking for us."

"They won't find you here, though," said Jake, in quite a menacing tone. "They'll be looking down the river for you, and while they're doing that, I will take the rest of the silver and disappear, start a new life for myself abroad, where no one will find me. Not quite how I wanted to end things here, but you have forced my hand. Even if I don't get it all away, I've got plenty away already, enough for a fresh start I reckon."

"The only new life you deserve is one behind bars!" shouted Liz, breaking down in tears at the man she'd admired so much turning out to be no better than a common thief.

Jake moved towards her, but James stood in front of her. "Leave her alone," he said, protectively. "She's done nothing to you."

"You have almost ruined my plans, my future," said Jake, then seemed to calm as Liz continued her loud sobs. He crossed to another small vault the children had not yet explored and produced from it a length of thin rope.

"Get in there," he ordered, pointing to the small vault the four had tried to hide in.

They did as they were instructed and Jake made them all sit down on the stone slab. It was very cold, but no one dared to complain.

Jake began to wrap rope around Barrie's wrists then suddenly stopped. "Phones," he barked. "Give me your mobiles now. I'm not having you phoning for help."

The children, rather reluctantly began to delve into their pockets. Barrie, Jenny and James each held out their mobile phones. Liz meanwhile had pulled up her trouser leg and seemed to be scratching at her calf.

"Come on. Come on," barked an irritated Jake. "You have one I know, stop messing about."

"Sorry, my leg was just so itchy," she said, hurriedly holding out her phone. Jake took it and one by one turned each device off.

"Not having any trackers on these things giving the game away," he said, seeming quite proud of his own foresight. He put them on the floor by the entrance, then continued with his task of tying up the four.

"Wrists and ankles should sort you out," he said. "There is only me working here today, so no point in shouting, no one will hear you. If you do, mind, I'll gag you. Do I need to now?"

They all shook their heads and Jake, seeing an iron ring in the wall, ran the rope through, tying them up to that also.

Taking their phones, Jake left them, in near darkness, save for their torches which he had let them keep, and hurried up the steps out of the ice house.

"Crikey, we are in a fix." said James, trying not to sound defeated. "What are we going to do?"

"Not as much of a fix as we might be," replied Liz, in an excited voice, "I didn't get all my apps transferred, and thought I'd do some while we picnicked."

"What's that got to do with this?" asked Jenny. James grinned, he thought he knew.

"I had both my phones with me still. I gave Jake my old phone, the one without the sim card, and hid my new one down my sock, just in case he had us empty out our pockets. I wasn't scratching my leg, I was hiding my phone! I had to quietly turn it off in case it got a message and made a noise!"

"Fantastic!" squealed Jenny in delight. "You're a genius. We can phone for help. Can you reach it?"

"Shh!" interrupted Barrie, his sharp ears had heard something.

They all fell silent and, sure enough, there was the sound of feet coming down the steps in the entrance to the ice house. Jake reappeared, with some lengths of strong chain and padlocks.

"Not going to chance you escaping," he said, as he disappeared down the tunnel towards the kayaks. There was a clang as the metal gate was banged shut, and the sound of chain being wrapped around it. Jake reappeared, still looking angry and, without another word, crossed back to the main entrance, pausing to close and secure that gate also, before disappearing up the steps.

Barrie held his hand up to stop anyone from talking and cocked his head on one side, listening hard. There was the sound of the chain being wrapped around the top entrance gate, and then silence.

"He's gone," Barrie said. "Right then Liz, can you get to your phone?"

Liz wriggled, reaching down with her bound hands. They all had to reach down as Jake had used one rope to bind them all.

"I, I just have to reach down the back of my sock." she panted, shuffling her feet back towards her as she bent her knees up.

"I, yes. Got it." she said, beaming triumphantly. "We'll soon be out now!"

The others all let out relieved little laughs. They had all wanted an adventure, and to solve the mystery, but it had been very frightening to be captured, and James felt they were in real danger. Jake had looked wild, and he was sure, would stop at nothing to make good his escape.

"Call Dad. He'll know what to do," suggested Barrie, as Liz turned the phone on, and reeled off his father's mobile number. Liz dialled, with trembling fingers, the phone clamped between her bound hands. She pressed the loudspeaker button, as it would be too difficult trying to hold the phone to her ear, and they all waited, impatiently, for the call to connect.

Without a single ring, the phone returned to the dialling screen. Liz gave a frustrated exclamation.

"What's wrong with it? It's a new phone!" she protested.

Barrie, leaned over to see the screen. "There's nothing wrong with your phone," he answered, pointing to the top of the screen. "It's just out of signal. We should have expected it would be. You know how dodgy reception is up at the farm, let alone underground."

Liz looked crestfallen, her shoulder slumped. She had been so sure that she'd save the day with her phone that the disappointment was too much and a tear ran down her cheek.

"Try the emergency number," suggested James, not ready to give up hope just yet.

"What good will that do?" asked Liz, cuffing away her tears. "It's out of range, look."

"Dad told me once that all the mobile phone service providers share masts for emergency calls, so all we need is for any provider to have, even weak coverage here, and we're saved."

Liz looked doubtful.

"It's worth a try," encouraged Jenny, and so Liz again began to dial.

Alas she had the same result as before. Trapped underground in North Wales, they had no mobile signal whatsoever.

"Better put your phone away in case Jake sees it," said Barrie, "We don't want to get him any angrier."

Jenny pushed her head against Liz's shoulder in a friendly nuzzle.

"It was a really good idea to keep the phone and try it. I don't know how you thought so quickly to hide it so well, I was far too scared to even think straight."

Liz smiled, grateful for Jenny's kind words.

"You would have thought of it, in my position," she said, leaning back into Jenny.

"Well, what shall we do now?" asked James.

"There's not a lot we can do," said Barrie. "We can't really play I spy, there's nothing to look at!"

James chuckled, attempting valiantly to keep everyone's spirits up.

"Look on the bright side. You'll be able to write a fantastic story based on this when we get out, Jen."

"If we ever do get out," muttered Liz, under her breath.

The time passed slowly. It was so very cold for the four in the ice house, tied up, they couldn't move to stay warm, so instead huddled together as best as they could.

On Barrie's suggestion, they had switched off three of the four torches to save the batteries, not knowing how long they would be held prisoner for, but aware that being in complete darkness would be a very miserable experience indeed.

Lunchtime came and went. The four, despite their fear, began to feel very hungry.

"Should we call Jake and ask for our food, do you think?" asked Jenny, whose stomach was feeling very empty indeed.

James considered, "No, I think we will just have to go hungry. We can ask him when he next comes here, but I fear, if we call, he may think we were just calling for help. I don't know about you, but I don't fancy being gagged."

"You're right. I hadn't thought of it that way," said Jenny, and tried to think of anything but food.

They heard a generator start up, which was their only clue that Jake was still around. Three o'clock came and went and Barrie, noting the time, commented how his dad would soon begin looking for them.

"We'll never be trusted by him again," said James, hating to have broken his word about being at Barrie's nain's for no later than three.

"Don't be silly, of course we will. Dad will understand," said Barrie. "It's not like we're choosing to stay away."

"But won't they all be so worried. It's dreadful. I wonder if our parents will be contacted," said Liz, imagining her mother's worried face and feeling tears pricking at her eyes.

Barrie took charge, fearing everyone could soon start panicking.

"Let's just see what happens. It will all be ok. Dad will sort it."

"I do hope so," said Liz, and James agreed.

Jenny didn't answer and Barrie flashed his torch at her.

"You ok Jen? You're in a world of your own," he said, nudging her.

"Sorry, yes. I was just thinking about the silver and why the need for all those blue waterproof bags. Jake said he'd already taken some of the silver, do you think he took it in his van before it was noticed to be missing?"

"I have no idea," said Barrie. "But what I do know, is that he isn't to get away with any more. If we could only be untied, we could perhaps at least hide some of it. There must be small gaps we could slip tiny priceless items into."

The background hum of the generator stopped, and the four all strained their ears, listening for any sound to give them a clue as to what was happening above ground. Very faintly, they could just make out the sound of someone talking. Who this was and to who they were talking, no one could tell. The conversation lasted no more than a couple of minutes, then, after a minute or so of silence, right in the distance, they heard a car engine start.

"That's our car!" cried Barrie, "I recognise the tone! Something's happening then, I wonder if we've been missed already."

There came the rattle of the chain at the top gate and the four stopped talking as Jake, unlocking the second gate, entered the ice house.

"You've caused quite a stir," he said to the four, poking his head in at their small vault. "Gone on a picnic and not returned. See what trouble your meddling has caused."

"How do you know?" asked Barrie, not letting on he'd recognised the car.

"Sarah's just come to the Hall. Out of her mind with worry, she is, asking if I'd seen you, which of course I said I hadn't, and then pleading with me to join in the search party with the police and mountain rescue. They reckon you may have been swept down the river. Alan is already searching the banks for you."

Barrie's heart sank. Sarah had been so close. If only he'd shouted, they may all be safe now. He hated the worry this would be causing her and his dad.

"Naturally," continued Jake, "being the dependable, friendly bloke I am, I immediately agreed to stop working and join in the search, so you pests are costing me an evening wasted looking for you. Still, it will keep the police away from here and when the search is stood down, I'll return for what's mine."

"How long will you be gone for?" asked James.

"Till dark, I imagine, be suspicious for me to slip off early. Why?" Jake replied.

"It's just, we're freezing sitting so still, and Jenny's going mad with hunger. We have our picnic in the kayaks still. If you're going to be so long, could you at least untie us and leave us with our food? We didn't mean to cause all this trouble. We were only exploring, you'd have done the same I bet at our age."

Jake looked doubtful, so James continued, "And you've locked all the gates, there's no way we can escape. We would just be a little more comfy. Please?"

"Please Jake. I know you're not a bad man," added Liz, in a small voice, biting her bottom lip to stop from crying.

Jake didn't answer, though his expression had softened slightly. He turned and disappeared down the passage towards the kayaks. They heard him unlock the gate and he soon returned, carrying with him the bags containing their lunch.

"Will you please untie us?" asked James again, "We can't eat unless you do, and you know we can't escape. Please?"

Jake, still looking unsure, finally produced from his pocket a folding knife. He, rather roughly, cut the ropes bonding the hands and feet of the four.

"There," he said, as they massaged their sore wrists. "Now I must go and join in the search. I'll be back after dark. Don't try anything, or you'll be sorry." And with that, he was gone, locking the gates behind him. The four heard his van start up and pull away.

"Right, let's have something to eat and then set about exploring these vaults. We may be able to take the gates off their hinges or something," said Barrie. "Somehow or other, we just have to escape."

160

Chapter Eighteen

Liz's Bright Idea

The four eagerly opened the bags containing their picnic. The stress of being captured, as well as the cold temperatures, had left them feeling ravenous. They tucked in.

"I don't think I've ever tasted a nicer picnic," said James, taking another bite of his cheese and ham sandwich.

"Had we better try and make this food last, do you think?" asked Liz, taking an egg mayonnaise sandwich. "We don't know how long Jake will keep us here."

"He'll have to bring us food if we run out," said Jenny, whose rumbling tummy was at last calming with the very welcome food.

"He doesn't have to do anything," said Barrie. "He's not exactly playing by the rules now, is he?"

"No, and it would be so miserable to be stuck here all night with no food. I really do think we should save a sandwich each, and a brownie. It's a good job Sarah packed us so much up isn't it? There's enough to feed an army here," said Liz, and the others agreed, albeit Jenny somewhat reluctantly. Despite their predicament the children all thoroughly enjoyed the picnic, and felt a good deal better afterwards. Their hunger satisfied, the four were determined not to just sit and wait for Jake's return.

"Let's see if we can find a way out. We haven't explored any of this place, other than where the silver is kept. Who knows what else there may be," suggested Barrie.

"For all we know, the gates may lift off at the hinges," added James. "We could be out of here in a minute or two."

That motivated everyone into action, and they went to the gate that lead to the waterway.

Looking through the gate, by the light of her torch, to the kayaks, Jenny voiced what they were all thinking.

"How close they are, just sat, patiently floating, waiting to take us away to safety."

They certainly were tantalisingly close, Liz, the smallest, tried to squeeze through the gaps between the metal uprights in the gate.

"It's, no, good," she panted, "I get wedged, it's just too narrow."

Barrie and James were examining the hinges of the gate to see if there was any way they could open the gate at that end and escape. The hinges, alas, had large metal pins through the top, preventing the gates from being lifted up. It was very disappointing.

"I can't get the pin out." said Barrie. "It's too big to bend back straight by hand and slide out."

"We'll keep an eye out for any tools that we may be able to use to bend the pins. Who knows what Jake may have left here," replied James, "Come on. Let's check the other gate, then explore."

They all left the gate and crossed back through the main vault to the entrance gate. James and Barrie examined it gate in detail and declared it as formidable as the first gate.

"We're stuck here then," said Jenny.

"Unless we find a tool to remove the pins," said Barrie.

"Yes, let's explore. I can't wait to look into every bit of here," said Liz.

They turned their backs to the entrance gate and shone their torches round the main vault. They had been so rushed when they had first entered and then found the silver, that no one had taken much notice about the vault as a whole. The main vault was rectangular, beautiful, and very gothic, with its low, vaulted ceiling and stone flagged floor. There were six small vaults, or chambers, that led off from the main vault, three on each side and all with identical stone arches as doorways. The silver was in the middle vault on the right hand side, and Jake had tied them up in the farthest vault on the left hand side, just beyond which was the passageway they had come up from the water.

They split into pairs, the girls working clockwise from the entrance gate, the boys, anticlockwise. It was eerie, examining the small vaults by torchlight; their beams leaving strange shadows on the walls. Every child was keeping a sharp lookout for anything that may help them escape.

The four vaults they hadn't been in didn't contain anything of use, certainly no tools they could use to help them open the gates, and they all gathered in the vault containing the silver. There were four large crates, identical to the one Barrie had removed the silver snuff box from. Each filled with straw, no doubt protecting the valuable silver, hidden inside each crate. Piled in the corner were half a dozen or so waterproof blue bags, the four, examining them agreed they were the same, fold down style that the kayaking centre they'd visited on Monday used.

"I wonder what the need for those bags is," said James.

"Do you think Jake will transfer the silver to them and seal them to stop them from tarnishing?" asked Jenny. "It is quite damp in here after all."

James considered, "I don't think so. After all, you can polish silver bright again. A little tarnish isn't going to damage it."

Barrie moved the bags and, stuffed behind them in the corner, was a pile of small, air filled, plastic cushions.

"I've seen these things before," said Liz. "They are air pockets, used to protect items in the post and are lighter than wrapping things in blankets, and better for the environment than using polystyrene."

"So," said Barrie, slowly, voicing his thoughts as he looked at all in front of them. "Why, in an underground vault would you have waterproof bags and super light protective packaging? What are you doing with it Jake?" Barrie frowned in deep concentration and the other three sat in silence, all thinking hard.

The minutes ticked by.

Suddenly Barrie let out such an exclamation in the dimly lit silence that they all jumped.

"I've got it! I know how Jake is moving the silver!" he cried.

"How?" asked the other three. "Come on, tell us!"

"It's all falling into place," said Barrie, grinning at their impatient faces. "I believe Jake floats the silver, a couple of pieces at a time, out down the waterway and down the river. He could easily put a couple of items in, wrapped in the straw for protection and cushioned further by the air pockets which would help keep the bag afloat. Plus, he could trap air in the bag when he seals it."

"Gosh, yes!" said James, his eyes lighting up. "Jake, or another person in on this with him, could then fish the bag out from the water further downstream. What a genius idea!"

"It explains a lot," added Jenny. "Don't you remember, Bar, your dad remarking how calm and good tempered Jake was about being searched by the police, was it, three times? Jake, not only knew there was no silver in his van, but that he was managing to steal it and get it out from Tully Hall right under their noses. Good tempered? Jake must have been laughing himself silly inside, full of glee and pride at his own cunning."

"I do, yes," said Barrie. "You're right, and by being so helpful to everyone, friendly and smiley, he kept the suspicion from himself. Sarah said she couldn't believe Jake to be responsible."

"And," added Liz, who had been sat quietly. "It might explain why Jake flew off the handle when we said about kayaking down the river." Liz had been the most affected by Jake's outbursts so they had stayed in her mind. "He wouldn't have wanted us paddling down and coming across a blue bag now, would he?"

"Absolutely not," agreed Barrie, "and asking when you three went home. That told him when he could resume smuggling the silver away."

"Smuggling! It does sound so exciting when you call it that," said Jenny.

"Is it not exciting enough then?" laughed Barrie, and the others joined in, thrilled and elated at their solving of Jake's plot.

James brought them down to earth.

"We have done very well, figuring out Jake's plot, but, you know, we haven't managed to do anything to foil it; to stop him from stealing all the silver and making good his escape." The girls at that, looked more than a little downhearted.

"We will have to put our energy into escaping," said Barrie, determined not to give up and just stay a prisoner as all the silver is taken away in front of him. "I'm going to have another look at the gates." With that, he got up and, his head torch shining brightly, disappeared down the tunnel to the waterway.

James turned to Liz. "Can I borrow your phone please? I want to hold it up all round here and see if an emergency call will go through. It's our best chance of getting help, being rescued, and stopping Jake taking the silver."

Liz fished the phone out, which had still been stuck down her sock and handed it to him,

"You're the tallest, so you can reach highest. Your long arms will be halfway up the entrance steps if you shove them between the bars of the gate." said Liz. James smiled and, taking the phone, headed into the main vault and towards the entrance.

There came the sound of Barrie rattling the waterway gate, and James humming contentedly as he walked round the ice house, painstakingly trying to call the police from every corner. Jenny and Liz remained by the silver. They had taken one of the blue waterproof bags each to sit on, trying to insulate themselves from the cold coming through the stone flagged floor. With no obvious way they could help Barrie or James, Jenny and Liz set about exploring the contents of the crates.

Carefully, one crate at a time, working by torchlight, they removed the antique silver objects, placing them gently on the floor by the crate they had been removed from. They both were over awed at the beauty and marvelled at the workmanship and skill involved in each and every piece.

"All of this will have been handmade," said Liz, carefully taking a matching pair of silver table salts, each bearing the family crest the four had seen on the snuff box and in the entrance to Tylluan Hall. "Look, these even have their blue glass liners to protect the silver from the salt."

Jenny looked with interest. She didn't have the knowledge about antiques that Liz had gained from her mother, but could still appreciate the quality and beauty in the items. Working quietly, the two emptied each crate. The little room shone with reflected light from the silver in the light Jenny's torch. Soon there was a collection of over 60 pieces of precious silver on the floor; there were all sorts of things, from large, beautifully decorated, heavy candlesticks, cutlery, picture frames, inkwells and stands, snuff boxes, vestas, pocket watches and chains, right down to a tiny silver box with a gold coloured grill inside. It was less than three centimetres long and looked so delicate, Jenny wondered how it survived in such perfect condition all these years. Liz informed her it was a vinaigrette, and would have been filled with a pleasant perfume under the grill, to mask the less pleasing odours of Victorian life.

"This must be worth…" began Jenny, examining the little box.

"A fortune," finished Liz. "A lot of these pieces, as Sarah said, are one offs, irreplaceable. This collection is, well, priceless."

James appeared, with Barrie at the entrance to the silver store.

"It's no use," said James, holding up Liz's phone. "I've tried everywhere, and Bar's helped me, no signal on any network at all."

"Zip. Nada. Nothing. And no luck with the gates either," added Barrie, "neither of them would budge an inch."

"Rats," said Jenny. "We're stuck here then, and all this lovely silver will be taken away forever. Come and have a look at it, you two, it really is stunning."

"Can I please have my phone back? I want to photograph the silver, so at least there's a record of what was here if Jake manages to take it away."

"That's a good idea," said James, handing Liz her phone. "We'll use our torches to light up the silver, the flash on your phone will likely cause a glare reflection and you won't see anything."

A photoshoot began and, with the help of the others, Liz took many photographs, recording every item of silver in the ice house. Pleased with her efforts, but stiff from being sat relatively still in the cold, Liz stood up, allowing the boys to look properly at the silver as Jenny began to put some of it carefully back into the crates. The boys were as impressed as the girls had been, and just as frustrated that the silver may soon be lost.

Liz, standing in the stone archway, looking at the silver sighed, and her gaze fell to the blue bag she had been sitting on, and that now, her phone was lying on. An idea began slowly rolling round in her mind. She looked hard at her phone and the bag, as her thoughts gradually began to take shape.

"I don't suppose... You'll think I'm mad, but I don't suppose we could float my phone down the river in a blue bag, and get it to make a noise, an alarm or something, could we?"

The three looked at her in complete admiration.

"Liz! You aren't mad, you are a blooming genius!" shouted Barrie.

"Brilliant" added James, his mind beginning to focus on how to make the plan work. "We can set a repeating alarm to go off. I can power save to make it last longer. What a great idea! Well done!"

Liz looked a little embarrassed, and Jenny gave her friend a squeeze.

"You are super smart," she said, proud of Liz.

"Right," said Barrie, picking up a bag. We can fill the bag with air pockets, and put the phone in the middle. It shouldn't sink if we get the seal right.

Liz looked a little apprehensive at the mention of the phone sinking. She hadn't thought that she may possibly lose her precious new phone. Barrie saw her doubtful face and sought to reassure her.

"It will float, and it really is the only possibility we have of getting rescued and saving the silver."

"Why don't we practice with another bag first?" suggested Jenny, desperate for the plan to work and for the silver to be saved. "We could tie a rope to it and throw it through the bars of the gate. That way, we can pull it back to us as many times as we need until we know it will definitely float and that we can throw it far enough. It will have to be thrown hard enough to clear the walkway and the kayaks. Can you imagine how frustrating it would be if we threw Liz's phone and it only landed on the stone ledge, or in a kayak?"

The others all groaned. That didn't bear thinking of. It would truly be awful.

"That's an excellent idea," said Barrie, picking up a blue bag. "Pass me some air pockets, Jenny."

Jenny passed Barrie the pockets and, together, they went to collect some rope and on to the waterway gate to practice. James and Liz stayed in the silver vault, working out what to do on Liz's phone.

James first removed the security from the phone, so anyone could access it. Liz then wrote a welcome note, which would be the first thing that anyone accessing the phone would see, it read:

169

WE ARE PRISONERS IN THE ICE HOUSE AT TYLLUAN HALL. JAKE, THE BUILDER, HAS LOCKED US INSIDE. HE HAS STOLEN THE SILVER. PLEASE CALL THE POLICE IMMEDIATELY. LIZ, BARRIE, JENNY & JAMES

Liz had gone to where Barrie and Jenny were tying the rope to the bag by the gate, to check the spelling of the Hall. Realising they didn't know Jake's surname, she hoped "The builder" would be enough for the police.

She took the phone back to James who took a photograph of her and him holding the silver candlesticks and set it as the phone's wallpaper, in an effort to demonstrate to whoever found the phone that it was genuine, and it was an emergency.

James then set about the alarm. He picked the most shrill alarm tone and turned it up to maximum volume, it was really quite unpleasantly loud in the confines of the vault. "I'll set it to repeat every two minutes. It sounds for a full minute, I can't get it to go continuously, but someone should surely hear that, the bag won't be travelling that quickly." James had labelled the alarm "ICE HOUSE T HALL CALL POLICE" which would flash on the screen as the alarm sounded, in case someone who didn't know about smartphones found the bag.

"I'll activate it by the gate, just before we put it in the bag. No point in deafening us in here. I've disabled all your other apps for now, Liz, to maximise the battery life. It's on 37%, so won't last forever, but should last a good while."

He and Liz took the phone through to where Barrie and Jenny were, by the gate. Jenny greeted them.

"I'm a rubbish shot!" she said, "I tried and two out of three times, the bag landed on the walkway, the other time it ended up in your kayak. Bar's getting a bit better."

They all watched as Barrie, his body pressed against the gate, with his right arm through the bars, holding the top of the bag, swung the bag back and forth a few times before throwing it towards the water. Splash! The bag landed neatly in the water and Jenny quickly put her foot on the rope coil at Barrie's feet that was rapidly being pulled through the gate. Barrie bent and picked up the rope, pulling the bag back out of the water and through the gate.

"Once more for luck," he said and again threw the bag. Barrie had misjudged slightly, and the bag landed on the walkway about an inch from the water. It was tantalisingly close, but they all imagined just how horrendous it would be if that bag had the precious phone in it.

Barrie growled and yanked the bag back in.

"The wet rope makes it harder," he said. "Put the phone in and seal it up tight. I'll get it in the water."

James took the bag and, activating the alarm in Liz's phone to go off in five minutes then in two minute intervals thereafter, he put it carefully in the bag, held securely between the air pockets, and folded the top of the bag down several times, clipping it shut.

"There, it's in and should be watertight," he said, handing the bag to Barrie. "Good luck."

"Cross your fingers," said Barrie, with a nervous grin, squeezing the taut bag between the bars of the gate.

The other three all crossed their fingers, Liz crossed her toes as well to bring a little extra luck, as Barrie began to swing the bag back and forth again, building up the momentum.

"I can't watch!" said Jenny, and closed her eyes.

Time stood still as Barrie, with a loud grunt of effort, let go of the bag, hurling it as hard as he could towards the water.

It was a monumental effort, rewarded with a loud splash as the bag landed hard on the water.

Jenny opened her eyes and they all held their breath as Barrie's head torch scanned the water for the bag. Had it sunk? It was nowhere to be seen!

As quickly as it had disappeared it reappeared, bobbing up to the surface and began to move slowly downstream. The four all breathed great sighs of relief.

"Good luck little phone," called Liz to the bag and the others joined in. All their hopes now rested on that phone reaching someone safely, and the finder knowing what to do. The four could do nothing but wait.

Chapter Nineteen

Rescue

It didn't take long for the bag to float out of sight, disappearing into the darkness of the waterway.

"Well, it's gone," said James, "I hope it stays afloat."

"Yeah, I hope it doesn't get hooked up on anything," said Jenny

"How can it?" said Barrie, who didn't want to engage in any negative thoughts. "There's nothing really sticking out on the bag, and the walls of the passageway are smooth. There's nothing to stop it making it all the way to the river. The brick wall won't snag it, and then the current will push it into the middle."

"Shall we wait and listen for the alarm?" asked Liz, keen for any confirmation that her phone was still working, not lying at the bottom of the channel of water.

"There's no point," said James. "It has got five minutes until it goes off for the first time. It should have made it to the river in that time. At any rate, it will be out of earshot.

Liz gazed, somewhat wistfully into the dark down the waterway. She fervently hoped that wasn't the last time she would see her phone.

"Come on Liz," called Jenny, jerking Liz from her private concerns. "I'm going to pack the rest of the silver back up. Come on and we'll do it together, you can help me find the hallmark things you spoke of."

Liz turned and followed Jenny through towards the main vault. James watched them go, smiling as he realised how

Jenny was, very skilfully, distracting Liz from worrying about her phone. They really did all seem to get on so well, he just hoped they all got out of this ok.

Jenny and Liz packed the rest of the silver carefully away. They didn't know really why they did it, when it would make it easier for Jake to take away, but it seemed wrong to leave it lying on the floor where it could so easily be damaged.

The boys, with no phone to try reaching the police with, and no tools to work on the gates, sat in the vault where they had been tied up.

"I wonder how Dad is, and Sarah, and Nain. They will be going out of their minds with worry," said Barrie, hating the thought of causing distress to the people he loved.

"I wonder if our parents have been told," said James, "Dad would have faith in me, I reckon, but Mum would be beside herself."

"Well, there really is nothing we can do but wait," said Barrie, looking up as Jenny and Liz entered the small room. They flopped down beside the boys.

"How long do you think till we're rescued?" asked Liz, who had supreme confidence in her plan working.

"It depends how fast the river is flowing and how far down it they are searching. That's if," James cut Barrie off, not wanting Barrie to say "if it worked at all." Liz was being so brave, James didn't want her worrying any more than necessary.

"It could be an hour or two I'd imagine, maybe a little longer."

"Well, in that case, shall we have some more of the picnic?" suggested Jenny.

"Why not," said James, crossing his fingers that they weren't going to spend a hungry night there.

Jenny handed round a sandwich and a chocolate brownie to everyone and, with two torches stood like candles, they enjoyed a second picnic in the near darkness. Although they were not as ravenous as they had been earlier in the day, it helped to pass the time and, eating slowly, they chatted about the situation they'd landed in.

"Whatever happens, there's one thing I know," said Barrie,
"What's that?" asked Jenny, nibbling on her chocolate brownie

"We did what we set out to do! We, us four, have solved the mystery of Tully Hall! We did it!"

The others all began to smile and were soon beaming at each other with pride. In the drama of being captured and working on escaping, they hadn't really realised the significance of what they had found, not only the silver, but how it got there, and by who. The mystery was indeed solved.

"It will make a great story for school. I bet we'll have to write about what we did in our summer holidays," said Jenny, who was already planning in her head how she would tell the story. "I bet no one would believe us"

An hour passed by, with the four taking it in turns to walk around the vault, just to keep a little warmer.

"It's a good name, the ice house," said Liz. "I feel like a block of ice, I can't even feel my feet," she added, stamping them on the ground.

James, who'd been sat quietly, looked concerned. Liz, catching sight of his frown by the light of her torch, said "Don't look so worried James, my feet won't fall off!"

"Sorry," said James, "I was thinking."

"What is it?" asked Barrie, "You look really serious."

"Well, I don't want to worry you, but I've been thinking."

"Go on," said Jenny, impatiently, worried by James' tone.

"Jake is helping with the search for us, or at least pretending by going along."

"Yes…" said Jenny, as Barrie's hand flew to his mouth, guessing what James was about to say.

"What if it's Jake who finds the phone in the bag?" said James. They all sat in horrified silence. They had been so sure that the phone would lead to their rescue, they could hardly comprehend how, rather than that, it could place them in even more danger.

"If Jake finds it, we're in big trouble." said Barrie, voicing what they were all thinking. "He'd be furious. Heaven knows what he would do to us, but I can't think it would be pleasant."

"What shall we do?" asked Liz, her voice trembling.

"I've been thinking about that for the last half an hour," said James, "and I think I have a plan.

The others waited in silence as James got his thoughts together.

"I think we should hide in the vault nearest the entrance, right at the back of it. Then, if Jake comes in, we can make a dash for the exit and get out. He can't chase all four of us, so one of us at least must surely be able to escape and run up to the farm."

"We could leave a torch on in this vault, so it looks like we're in here," said Jenny.

"Good idea," said James, nodding.

"I don't like it. I don't like us maybe getting split up and one or more of us stuck with a very angry Jake."

"Neither do I really, Bar," said James. "But I don't think we have a choice. If you can think of a better plan?"

Barrie couldn't, nor could either of the girls, and so, leaving Jenny's torch facing the back wall, they left the picnic bags and moved to the vault nearest to the entrance gate. The tension was mounting and they stood in silence in the dark, waiting to see if anyone would come.

Time ticked slowly on.

"Can you hear my heartbeat?" whispered Liz.

Jenny, who was holding her hand, both to comfort Liz and herself, whispered back. "No but I can barely hear anything with the blood rushing in my ears."

"Shh!" said Barrie, urgently. He'd heard something.

Jenny immediately stopped talking and the four stood in absolute silence, straining their ears to catch even the smallest of sounds. The tension was almost unbearable. Jenny could feel herself trembling, whilst James had a huge knot in his stomach. He let out a shaky breath.

Clink!

There! What was that sound? Petrified, the four pressed against each other in the pitch darkness.

Clink!

There it was again. It sounded like the chain at the top gate was being moved.

The glow of a torch could be made out on the steps, and James pulled them all deeper into the back of the vault. It was evident, someone was entering the ice house, but who? Footsteps sounded on the stone steps, echoing into the vaults. The four stood motionless, pressed against the back of the vault, frozen in fear. The torchlight flashed around as whoever was holding it came to the second entrance gate. The four, hearing the chain rattle, all held their breath.

"Get ready to run," whispered James. Liz wasn't sure her legs would be able to walk, let alone run.

The children, listening hard, heard not one, but two voices, talking in hushed tones, was it Jake with reinforcements?

The gate opened with a slight creak and powerful torch light shone into the main vault. There'd be no chance of escaping unseen, they'd just have to hope that at least one of them was too quick for Jake.

As they heard the footsteps pass through the gate into the main vault the children edged round in the darkness, ready to make a desperate run for it as soon as the footsteps went further in.

Just a few more steps, thought Barrie. Just a few more steps.

"Police!" shouted a voice, so suddenly, and so loudly, that the four all jumped and Jenny cried out in surprise.

"Kids? Are you here?" continued the voice, the beam from the powerful torch now pointing in their direction.

"Yes! Yes! We are!" they all shouted, immense relief washing over them that it wasn't Jake and that they were, at last, safe.

"Are you ok? It's all right, you're safe now." Entering the small vault and shining the torch away from their eyes, two figures stood in the dim light. Barrie recognised the strong welsh accent as belonging to the sergeant who had spoken with his dad and Jake during the excitement of the road block, almost a week ago. In his hand, he held a pair of bolt croppers.

"We're ok. We're fine." said James, speaking for them all.

Liz, overcome, had sunk to the floor, tears rolling down her cheeks. It had all been too much.

The sergeant tried to use his radio, but it wouldn't work underground, so he spoke to the officer behind him in urgent tones. That officer nodded, and ran back up the steps to get above ground. He returned a few minutes later, and spoke quietly to his sergeant.

"We've just let your parents know you are found Barrie, worried they were, we all were!"

"Sergeant, you have to get hold of Jake, he's behind this," began James, knowing from tales his father had told him, just how quickly criminals could disappear.

"Don't you worry, son. Part of that message I had passed confirmed to the officer who was near to Jake to arrest him. Now, let's get you above ground and somewhere to warm up."

The four, shepherded by the two policemen, walked up the stone steps, surprised to see it was getting quite dark. Vehicles could be heard roaring up the mountain road and, as the sergeant lead them around the side of the Hall, towards his car, Barrie waved madly at his father's car, which was racing down the drive towards them. It skidded to a halt by the four, throwing up stones, and Alan and Barrie's nain, along with Dash, all jumped out and ran to Barrie, enveloping him in a hug. Dash barked and jumped up at Barrie, pushing her nose at him. Alan opened his arms, gesturing to the other three and the adults embraced the four children tightly. Nain had tears streaming down her face, and was talking rapidly in Welsh, a thing she did when she was stressed. The sergeant spoke to her in Welsh and then, in English, said they should all go up to the farm and hear exactly what had gone on. The parents of Liz, Jenny and James had been told their children were safe and would be able to speak to them after the police had heard their story.

Another police car had arrived and, after a brief conversation with them, the sergeant told the children to get in any vehicle that had room in it, and they would all head up to Pen Y Bryn. They did as instructed, leaving two police officers behind by the ice house.

179

Up at the farmhouse, everyone piled into the large kitchen. Sarah hugged Barrie so tightly he squeaked as he hugged her back. Extra chairs and boxes were found to sit on and, over steaming mugs of tea, the children were asked to tell their story.

They took it in turns to tell it, beginning with how Jake's reaction to them being on the river had been strange, and how he had shouted with rage when they had asked to go into the ice house. A constable scribbled notes quickly into a book while they spoke. When Jenny said how she had then seen Jake going into the ice house and how it had raised their suspicion, the sergeant grinned. Nothing would get past these four, he thought, they were sharp. They continued with their story, and when Barrie said how much of the silver was still in the ice house Sarah gave a whoop of delight. She was shocked at learning Jake was responsible for the theft, but overjoyed to learn that it was safe.

"Wonderful!" she cried. "Shall we bring it out tonight?"

The sergeant smiled but shook his head. "We have the ice house under guard tonight, do not worry. We will bring it out in the daylight with our crime scene investigators overseeing and recording it all."

The children continued with their tale, of paddling up the passageway, their capture and frustration at the phone having no signal. They stopped where they had watched the phone and bag float away into the darkness.

"That was a remarkably clever thing to do. Really inspired." said the sergeant and now, it was his turn to tell the four what had happened next.

"We had been out searching for you with Mountain Rescue and any volunteer we could find. No one could understand how both the kayaks had disappeared, and it was feared they had taken on water and sunk. I had returned upstream to speak with your nain, Barrie, to reassure her. I had asked her to wait at her cottage you see, in case you phoned or turned up there. There I was stood on the bridge, speaking to your nain who was sat on her landing stage by the river when all of a sudden Dash started barking and looking upstream."

Dash, hearing her name, wagged her tail.

"Well, I ran round into the garden and down to the water's edge. Dash was still barking and I could see what had got her so excited. A blue bag was floating down the river, with an alarm sounding from it. I didn't know what to make of it, I can tell you. I grabbed a rake and, as the bag floated into range, I hooked it with the rake and pulled it out of the river. I had no idea what would be inside, and opening it, I took out your phone, still with its alarm sounding and 'Ice house, T Hall, call Police' was flashing. I then saw your message proper, and it's a good job I did. Jake, you see, was out helping us to search for you, the sly fella, and would probably be stood near one of my officers. I was just about to shout over the radio about the ice house when I noticed his name in your message."

"Crikey, he would have heard it!" said Barrie. "How did you stop him hearing?"

"That was the easy bit then," said the sergeant. "We have a code that tells officers to get themselves in a position where no one else can overhear them. When they confirm they are so, I pass my message. I told my team that PC Morgan and I were heading to the Hall, and for the officer nearest Jake not to let on, but not to lose sight of him, and be ready to arrest him if I said. When we found you, I got PC Morgan to give the go ahead for the arrest and Jake is now safe in custody. Let's see how he enjoys a little time behind bars, although it'll be warmer than what he subjected you poor things to."

Sarah poured everyone more tea and the sergeant continued, "Ran rings round us, he has. A clever but wicked man. Not clever enough for you four though, you saw through him. Fancy, here a week and you solve a mystery we haven't been able to for months, and recover priceless silver. We should sign you up to be cops!"

The four grinned with pleasure at the sergeant's, evidently heartfelt, praise.

"You all deserve a reward or recognition," he said. "But tell me, whose genius idea was it to float the phone down the river?"

Barrie, James and Jenny all looked at Liz.

"It was," began James,

"A team effort," cut in Liz, "It was a team effort."

The other three beamed at her. They were indeed a team, and a team they would stay.

Well, that has been the first adventure the four friends; Jenny, James, Barrie and Liz have shared. Somehow, I don't think it will be their last.

Printed in Great Britain
by Amazon